# I HAVE A
# PURPOSE

Carmen Ashe

Book design by Atomic Visual

ISBN: 0692836055
ISBN-13: 9780692836057
Library of Congress Control Number: 2017902708
CreateSpace Independent Publishing Platform
North Charleston, South Carolina

# DEDICATION

After my mother passed, three women in particular stepped into the void she left by continuing to shape me with their wisdom, love, and constant honesty—whether I wanted to hear it or not. You all treated me like a daughter and never once made me feel as if I didn't belong.

**Mrs. J**—During the course of writing this book, I lost Mrs. Johnson—or, as I called you, Mrs. J. I now have another angel watching over me. You were my best friend's mother, but more than that, you were another mother to me. I miss everything about you, Mrs. J, especially our long conversations. Thank you for your lessons.

**Pat**—I was a young girl when I applied for a position at your office. Who would have thought this relationship would evolve into a mother-daughter dynamic? Thank you for always believing in me, for never judging me, and for continually accepting my family and me as we are. You took the time to become my mentor without even knowing it. I learned a tremendous amount from you and am forever grateful for your teachings. You opened your heart and your family to me, and I am blessed to have met your mother and father. Your son became my brother, and I thank him for sharing you, his beautiful mother, with me. I love you always.

**Ginger**—Where do I begin? You taught me about everything from electrical panels and plumbing to how to handle various situations. One of the most valuable lessons was talking to me about your mom's writing and how she found that writing things down could be therapeutic. I took your mom's words of wisdom and put together paper and pen. I hope I have made you proud. Thanks also to Julie for having a daughter who is far beyond her time. I love you always.

I would like to dedicate this book in particular to those who are experiencing seemingly insurmountable obstacles in their lives. Never give up on yourself. Believe that everything happens for a reason. You may not understand why at the moment, but please realize that your journey through life holds a lesson for you. Please don't ever forget to laugh, and try to stay true to yourself no matter what.

# CONTENTS

# CHAPTER ONE

"You came into this world fighting," my mother said. "Even before you were born, no one could tell you what to do."

I was twelve years old the first time my mother told me the story. We were sitting in our small kitchen in the New York City apartment my parents had called home since 1963. I remember that the room always smelled like beans. My mother used them in most of her recipes, partly in an attempt to keep in touch with her Puerto Rican roots. I hated beans. The smell, though, wasn't enough to keep me away from the kitchen, which was my favorite room in the house.

In our apartment, my father's word was law. He was the breadwinner and the rule maker, both judge and jury. My mother, like the rest of us, was one of his subjects. But not in the kitchen. That was her kingdom.

We sat at the scarred kitchen table, surrounded by the familiar smells of beans and pork, as my mother told me about the first fight I ever won. She was quiet, almost apologetic, as she explained the circumstances of my birth.

"I'd already had your two brothers and your sister. I came from a family of sixteen, and I knew how much work having that many children could be. I told myself, 'Three's a good number.' So I went to the doctor and asked to have my tubes tied." Noticing my confused look, she explained, "It's a surgery that makes it so you can't get pregnant again."

"Because you didn't want to have any more babies?"

She shook her head. "I didn't see how I could take care of any more children. Your father…" She trailed off, seemingly reluctant to speak a word against her husband, although I knew what she meant. He provided the money, and it was my mother's job to take care of everything else. My family was Catholic, and very traditional. Dad was never very involved in our daily lives, because he felt child-rearing to be women's work.

"But you did have more," I pointed out.

My mother nodded. "First I had Richie." Richie was my youngest brother: only ten months older than I was. I could see where this story was going. "When I found out I was going to have another baby, I was shocked. What happened? I signed all the papers, and

I went in for surgery. What surgery did they do? I don't know. Whatever they did, it didn't work."

Even at twelve, I understood at least part of the problem: my mother's English wasn't the best. Something must have gotten lost in translation with the English-speaking doctors.

"I felt sick around Halloween, about five months after your brother was born," my mother said. "I thought I was getting a cold. Maybe one of the older kids brought it home from school, I thought. The weather was getting cooler. I went in for a checkup."

I could tell she was drawing the story out, so I said, "It was me, right?"

"I should have known, after four babies, what pregnancy was like." She shook her head ruefully.

"Then what?"

My mother swallowed. I wondered, then, what she would look like in confession. A little sad. A little guilty. Extremely repentant.

"It wasn't that I didn't want you," she said. "I didn't know you yet. Now that I know you, I love you, Carmen. You know that."

I did know that. My mother spoiled me. My sister thought I was the favorite, and I couldn't say I disagreed.

"When they told me I was pregnant again, I was devastated." Her voice got louder now, more emphatic. "Three children was enough work for me. Four was too much. Five? Five children, five mouths to feed, five college tuitions—do you understand?"

I understood. Our apartment wasn't meant to fit five kids, and I knew it. We were like too many peas in too small a pod.

"I never would have had an abortion. I never would have even considered it. God never would have forgiven me. I never would have forgiven myself."

I knew about sin. Even at twelve, I also knew about forgiveness and how hard it could be to earn forgiveness. Sometimes people did things they couldn't ever make up for, no matter what they said or did.

"Accidents, though, can happen," my mother said, quieter again. "I started to have a lot of accidents. I tripped a lot. I fell. I threw myself on the floor. A few times, I even punched myself in the stomach." My mother didn't cry when she said this. It was as if she were reciting a shopping list as she ticked off the reasons I might not have been born. I looked down at the kitchen floor and tried to imagine my pregnant mother deliberately sprawled on the linoleum.

"But you still had me," I said.

"I realized you were going to happen whether I wanted you or not," she said, "so I stopped having accidents. I thought I was done having children, but God wanted you here. There must be a reason you had to be born, Carmen. You have a purpose. I don't know what it is, but I know you have one, because you wanted so badly to be here—whether I was ready for you or not."

Some girls might have been hurt by this. They might have felt unloved. I'd grown up with my siblings, though, and I knew how difficult we all could be. Besides, my mother and I were very close. Maybe she spoiled me out of guilt, but there was still a lot of love between us.

I wasn't supposed to be born, but here I am. There must be a reason for it.

TONY, AS IT TURNS OUT, wasn't supposed to be born, either. When his mother was eight months pregnant, she said she felt sick. She stopped eating, and her belly became swollen and painful. "It's probably just from the pregnancy," she assured her husband. After all, stomach pains and an unreliable appetite were not unusual symptoms with a baby only a month away.

She didn't get better, though. The stomachaches turned into stabbing pains, and she developed a fever. When she experienced extreme bouts of nausea, her husband took her to the hospital from fear that something was wrong with the baby. He waited in the emergency room and prepared himself for news that his wife had miscarried; he tried to emotionally detach himself from his unborn son. He knew he'd have to be strong for his wife when he brought her home. She'd be devastated and would look to him for comfort.

The attending doctor came out to deliver an update. Tony's father, noting the man's clenched jaw, felt his heart sink. It was bad news. "Is it the baby?" he asked, already steeled for the worst.

"That's what I've come to ask you. Technically, aside from being premature, your son is fine. Your wife has appendicitis, and we'll have to operate to remove the inflamed organ. I'm afraid it's a rather dangerous operation, given the circumstances. We'll do what we can, though."

Tony's father was speechless. He'd been prepared to lose the baby, but he hadn't thought his wife would also be in danger.

"Before we start," the doctor said, "I want to ask you something." He took a deep breath and looked down at his shoes to steady himself. Tony's father waited for the question. "This is the situation, Mr. Ashe. When we go in to remove her appendix, we'll be dangerously close to the womb. I can either save the baby, or I can save your wife, but I can't save both. I realize this is a difficult choice, but we need to operate immediately or we'll risk losing them both."

Faced with the loss of his beloved wife or the loss of a stranger, the man who would become my father-in-law thought, *I don't know this boy. He hasn't even been born yet. I don't owe him anything.* "Save my wife," he said.

Miraculously, both Tony and his mother survived the appendectomy. Tony spent the first three months of his life undergoing treatments for pneumonia. He was monitored constantly to make sure his underdeveloped lungs were fighting off the infection with the help of antibiotics and breathing machines. For those three months, Tony was not allowed to leave the hospital. In the end, however, his parents took home a healthy baby—one the doctors had initially assured them would not live.

Tony and I wouldn't meet for years, but we already shared a story. Tony and I both had beaten the odds just by being alive. We were both fighters who'd arrived with a purpose.

# CHAPTER TWO

Tony and I collided in the spring of 1986. It was the year of the *Challenger* disaster, and life in New York City, and on planet Earth in general, presented me with quite a few personal challenges. I was nineteen years old and had learned to be careful around men.

The late-summer heat hadn't set in yet, and the day was warm enough for skirts and short sleeves but not so hot that my clothes stuck to me. My friend Liz and I were out for a joyride in her mother's car, as much to escape from our parents' apartments as to actually go anywhere. I had just moved back in with my mother and father, and none of us were very thrilled about my return.

It felt good to have some freedom for a little while. We passed a market on the corner, and Liz hit the brakes. "Oh!" she said. "Check *them* out."

I leaned around to see what had caught her attention. Two guys about our age sat in their car, deep in conversation, and they turned to look at us as we drove by. One lifted his eyebrows, sizing up Liz

"You're kidding," I told her.

She parked the car. "I am not. Which one do you like?"

"I don't know them."

Liz ignored me. "I like the younger one. What do you think?"

"You don't know them—that's what I think."

Liz swatted my arm, still making doe eyes at the two strangers. "Come on, Carmen. I'll teach you how to pick up guys."

"I don't need to pick up guys!" I insisted. "Men are trouble. Let's just go."

Liz clicked her tongue. "Fine. Stay in the car. I'm going." She reached for the door handle. I crossed my arms and flopped my head back against the headrest. "They're really cute," she said, drawing that last word out into a song.

I sneaked a peek over at the two young men inside the other car. She wasn't wrong.

"I'll just watch from here," I said.

Liz grinned at me. "Then you'd better take some notes."

Liz got out and took a few steps toward a nearby newsstand. She tossed her hair over one shoulder and waved with the tips of her fingers to the two men. The younger man said something to his companion—I guessed it was his brother—but they kept talking, no longer checking her out.

Liz tilted up her nose as if she didn't care. She walked to the newsstand and leaned on the counter, pretending to browse. Her posture definitely showed off her assets.

The guys still ignored her.

Liz muttered under her breath and then turned around, leaning on one elbow and putting the other hand on her hip.

The guys didn't notice.

Liz slid one hand under her hair, pulling it away from her neck and fanning herself as if the heat were too much to bear.

Nothing.

She dropped the act and scowled at them. The younger man—the one she'd had her eye on—flicked his gaze toward her before returning to the conversation with his brother.

Liz stomped back to the car, yanked open the door, and dropped into the driver's seat. "Oh, fuck him," she said. "He ain't all that."

I shot a parting glance toward the other car just as she reached for the ignition. "They're looking!" I hissed.

Liz leaned back against her seat to give the guys a long cool stare. The younger man was definitely focused on us, and his brother nodded encouragingly.

"He doesn't care about me," said Liz. "He's looking at you."

"Me?" I hadn't been the one swaggering and posing and making kissy lips.

As if he could hear us, the young man pointed to me and then gestured, *Come here*. He smiled and lifted his eyebrows. Liz was right—he was certainly the more handsome of the two.

I reminded myself how much trouble one man in particular had made for me lately. I shook my head, *No*.

He gestured again. *Pretty please?*

"What are you waiting for?" Liz snapped. "Go talk to him!"

"Don't you think I have enough men in my life right now?" I asked. "More men, more problems. You know I'm right."

"When *you* pick men, you pick trouble. This time, I'm picking for you. He's cute. He's interested. Go on."

I squinted at Liz.

"Fine," she said. "If you want to leave, we'll leave."

The guy, still smiling, now waved at me. *Please come talk.*

I figured he was a few years older, maybe mid-twenties, with a tightness of his jaw when he smiled—something a little strained, as if he were as wary of me as I was of him.

"I'm going to regret this," I said.

"No," Liz promised, "you're not." She gave me a little shove, and I reluctantly got out of the car.

I walked on heavy legs, dragging my feet and telling myself it would be smarter just to turn back and abandon this whole situation. I reminded myself that men could make my life miserable. *Haven't you learned anything?*

The guy got out of the car to meet me and reached for my hand.

I yanked it away before our fingers met. "Talk," I said firmly, "not touch."

The stranger grinned. "You're feisty."

"I am," I assured him, standing my ground. I didn't care that he was handsome. I made the rules, and if he didn't follow them, then I would get back in the car and go home. End of story.

He smiled again. "I like feisty, so let's talk. What's your name?"

"Carmen," I said.

"Carmen." He dipped his head in greeting. "Nice to meet you. I'm Tony."

"What are you doing out here?" I asked.

He frowned as if ashamed of himself, but his eyes glinted with humor. "My brother said he'd show me how to pick up girls."

*So I was right that they're brothers,* I thought. Out loud, I said, "Huh?" I glanced over my shoulder at Liz. "Funny." I leaned against the side of his car. His brother waved through the window, leaning over from the driver's seat. "Maybe he should chat up my friend," I suggested.

"Or maybe not," said Tony. "He likes you, too."

"But you're the one who waved at me."

His smile lit up his whole face. "I liked you more," he said.

"Because I'm feisty?"

"Of course." He wiggled his eyebrows, and I laughed.

"Then I should probably go," I said. "Liz will feel left out."

"I'd like to see you again," said Tony. "We could talk again sometime, maybe? Just talk, not touch." He flashed that grin again.

I hesitated. "I—"

"Can I just have your number? Then I can at least hear your voice. You don't even have to look at me."

After a moment's consideration, I gave him my number. "Say we're in class together if you call," I warned him. "My father doesn't like boys."

"What about men?" asked Tony.

"Men who want to hear his daughter's voice? Absolutely not."

"Sounds scary." Tony faked a shiver.

"Somehow I don't think that will slow you down."

His brother gave me a thumbs-up from inside the car. I turned to go, hiding a smile as I went. "See you around, Carmen," Tony said to my retreating back.

I headed back to Liz. "Well," I said, still grinning despite myself, "thanks for teaching me how to pick up guys."

She waved coyly at the car, where Tony and his brother were still watching us. "You learned from the best, honey."

It's hard now to say what made me walk over to that car. Tony's smile? His obvious interest? Chemical attraction? Or the sense that our stories were supposed to come together? Looking back, I'm sure I was fated to get out of that car, to cross the street to where he waited for me. Who would I have become if I'd ignored his gestures? What other path might my life have taken?

There is no other path. If I hadn't found him then, we would have met on another day. No version of my life story doesn't feature Tony. We were supposed to meet. I've known it since the first time we touched. I didn't feel much the moment he grabbed at my hand, but I did immediately afterward. I told him to keep his hands off me, and he did. He listened to me when I talked and respected what I said.

Plenty of other people in my life didn't.

When the phone rang the next afternoon, my mother answered it. She spoke a few clipped words into the receiver and then held it out to me. I took it from her, lifting it carefully to my ear. "Carmen speaking," I said.

A voice already becoming familiar said, "It's Tony… from yesterday."

My mother, silent, watched me. I fidgeted under her gaze, tethered by the phone cord, unable to escape for some privacy. "Yes," I said, "I remember you."

"I wanted to make sure you gave me a real number."

I turned away from my mother, but I still felt her stare boring into me. "Well, I guess I did."

"I'd like to take you out to dinner."

I turned back toward my mother. She hadn't moved. "All right," I said, "tomorrow." I gave him the address.

"I'll be there," he promised. "Looking forward to it, Carmen."

I smiled into the receiver. My mother didn't comment as I hung up the phone. "A new friend," I told her.

She examined me thoughtfully before saying, "I just hope you're careful this time."

It felt as though she'd stuck a pin in the happy bubble that had begun to fill me. I folded my arms. "I'm always careful," I assured her. It was true. In those days, I always was.

Some girls agonize over what to wear on a first date. They change their shoes, clothes, hair, and makeup again and again. I wasn't that kind of girl. A few minutes before Tony was supposed to pick me up for dinner, I was in my Levi's suit and waiting in the living room.

"Are you wearing that on a date?" demanded my sister, shockingly. .

I looked down at myself. It wasn't the sort of outfit Liz would pick for me, but I was never comfortable in dresses and heels. A pair of jeans and comfortable sneakers—practical, easy, and not fussy—were good enough for me. "What's wrong with it?"

"It's not very girly." She wrinkled her nose. "I don't know what he'll think."

"I don't care what he'll think," I told her. "This is what I'm wearing."

A knock came from the apartment door, and I went to answer it. When I opened the door and saw Tony on the other side, I laughed. Within seconds, he was laughing, too.

"What?" demanded my sister, coming to investigate. Tony stood on our doorstep wearing a Levi suit that matched mine exactly. She gaped at us each dressed in the same outfit and shook her head.

"We should take a picture," Tony said. He looked at me with a smile that didn't seem the least bit embarrassed.

I liked him before, but in that moment, I felt the connection between us—as if we were each holding the end of a long rope and little by little reeling each other in.

Talking to Tony came easily. Over dinner, in our matching Levi's suits, we started to get a feel for each other. Right away, Tony informed me, "I'm not the kind of man who likes to take care of a woman."

"Good," I said. "I'm not the kind of woman who likes to be taken care of."

"That's what I thought," Tony said with a grin. "Like I said…. you're feisty."

I shrugged this off, but I thought of my mother, who ran our household on the dollar-a-day allowance my father left her. I would never rely on a man like that. I would never give up the ability to take care of myself.

Most of our conversation stayed light, each of us keeping pace with the other's jokes. The territory between us felt balanced, and by the time he took me home, I was more than ready to plan a second date.

As we pulled up to my family's apartment, Tony suddenly got very quiet. He was silent as he parked; I had the impression he was preparing to tell me something important. "Hey, Carmen," he blurted out finally. "I need you to know something if we're going to see each other again." He seemed ready to reach for my hand again, but he stopped himself. It's strange how the fact that someone's respecting your rules can be as electric as a touch, but there it was.

Over dinner, Tony had been all easy smiles and wit, but suddenly he struck me as serious. "All right," I said, dreading what might come next.

He took a deep breath. "I have a daughter."

"Oh." I paused, caught off guard. That wasn't the sort of confession I'd expected at all. I could read the tension in his clenched jaw. His daughter mattered to him, I supposed, and if I didn't accept that, then there would be no place for me in his life. "OK," I said. He visibly relaxed at the ease with which I had taken this revelation. "Then there's something you should know about me, too," I said.

"All right."

"I have a stalker."

His eyes widened, but he considered this news in silence and finally said, "OK."

"An old boyfriend," I explained. "I've tried to get rid of him, but he won't leave me alone. He hangs around the apartment. He's threatened people. He gets…rough sometimes."

Tony fell silent again. That worried me. I liked Tony, but my ex had scared people away from me before. Maybe Tony would be scared off, too. He twisted in his seat to face me. "Are you serious about not wanting to be with this guy?"

"Yes!" I said, without hesitation.

"Then I'll get you out of it."

I sat back in my seat. "Just like that?"

"No woman deserves to be harassed. You don't need someone like that hanging around."

"No," I said, "I don't."

"So we'll get rid of him."

I gasped. I swallowed. At last I said, "I thought you don't like taking care of women."

Tony waved this away. "Protecting you isn't the same as taking care of you," he said. "If you could get rid of him yourself, you would have done it already. Let me help you," he said, insisting.

I nodded, still speechless. I'd fought my own battles for a long time. I'd fought that particular battle for the last two and a half years. What I needed right then was a hero, and by the time I got out of the car that night, it was starting to look like I'd found one.

# CHAPTER THREE

There hadn't been many heroes in my life. Mostly, when I'd needed saving, I'd had to save myself.

Tony and I had plenty to offer each other, but the first thing Tony ever offered me was safety, and that safety didn't come with a price tag. He didn't ask me to do anything for him to earn his protection. I didn't need to promise him anything. I didn't owe him anything. He'd see an injustice and want to make it right, whether it benefited him or not. Nobody had ever done something like that on my behalf.

I'd only had one serious boyfriend before meeting Tony, and he was Tony's opposite in every way. When I started going out with Cory, I considered myself special. My parents allowed me to date after I turned sixteen, and I was thrilled to have a real boyfriend, especially one who was so much worldlier than I was.

Most of Cory's friends ran with the cool crowd, and I wanted to belong to that world.

My parents were always very protective of me, as with every one of us kids, and looking back now I see that I was very naive. I daydreamed about Cory all the time and wrote his name in the margins of my notebook. I felt lucky he noticed me at all. He was also the first boy I ever slept with.

I got a lot of attention from boys, but I was never very flirtatious. Although I didn't think the same way my Catholic parents did, I wasn't very forward. My decision to get involved with Cory was anything but impulsive. I didn't let him pressure me into anything. Having sex was my choice. Far from feeling guilty about making that decision, I was overjoyed. Trust never came easily to me, and I was happy to have somebody I was comfortable with. I kept our relationship a secret from my family, because I knew my parents would be furious, but I couldn't keep my happiness a secret for long.

After we'd slept together, I bounced around the apartment for days, smiling to myself and laughing for what seemed no reason at all. I had no regrets. I also had no idea how much my life would change as a result of that one choice.

A few days after I'd slept with Cory, my sister came to visit. She had her own family by then, and unlike my parents and my brother Richie, who saw me every day, she immediately noticed the difference in my attitude. She cornered me in the room we'd once shared, arms crossed. "What's going on with you?" she demanded.

I could have denied that anything was happening, but I felt more generous than usual and wanted to share my happiness with my sister. I looked around to make sure no one else could hear and then lowered my voice to a whisper. "I…you know…with Cory."

"You what?" she demanded.

"I…we…" My religious family didn't spend a lot of time talking about the more physical aspects of romance, and when we did we were very solemn. I didn't know how to talk about my relationship, but I had to confide in somebody, and I trusted my sister. I knew she would be happy for me.

"You…" She raised her eyebrows.

"We…you know." I shrugged, grinning.

"Really?" In a disappointed tone.

"Really," I confirmed. "But it's a secret."

"Obviously." My sister mimed the motions of locking her lips and throwing away the key.

My father met me in the living room when I got home from school the next day. "You were out late," he said, instead of greeting me.

I felt suddenly wary. I gripped the straps of my backpack tightly with my fists. I said, "I'm trying to get a job," which was true. I spent some of my afternoon time filling out applications, although I usually made sure I had a chance to see Cory and his friends. They were becoming my friends, too, I thought. I was feeling like I fit in.

My father just kept sitting and watching me. The skin at the back of my neck started to crawl. "Your sister told me what you did," he said.

I bit my tongue to keep from saying anything. I could have called her a liar, but that would make me a liar, and my sister wasn't worth that. The anger pouring off my father practically choked me. I knew what he thought of girls who slept around. *It wasn't like that*, I wanted to tell him. *I didn't just sleep with anybody. I slept with* Cory. *You have no idea how happy it made me.* Yeah, I didn't think that argument would win my father over.

"I'm disappointed, Carmen," my father said, "but you know what happens now."

"I do?" Maybe he was going to hit me. Maybe he was going to ground me until I turned thirty.

My father nodded somberly. "You'll have to marry him."

I couldn't help myself. I laughed.

"This is not a joke!" My father slammed his fist down on the arm of the couch. "If you are willing to have sex with a man, then you must be willing to marry him."

"Are you kidding? I'm sixteen. I'm not marrying anybody."

"Then you shouldn't have slept with him," my father said, as if this were completely reasonable. He wasn't bluffing. He'd had the same conversation with my sister when she was my age and had had sex for the first time. My sister caved and did what my father had told her to do. She finally broke down and got married, and the marriage was not good. Even as a kid, I saw how unhappy she was. It occurred to me then that she'd probably told my father about Cory out of spite. Our old-fashioned father had forced her into a doomed marriage, and she must have resented my happiness. Since she was unhappy, she would try to make me unhappy, too. She must have assumed that I would make the same choice and bow to my father's wishes.

But I was not my sister. "Absolutely not," I said.

"Don't you love him?" my father asked. "Or will you just sleep with the first man who pays attention to you?"

I trembled with rage. Of course I was crazy about Cory, but that didn't mean I wanted to spend the rest of my life with him. My father gave me two choices: 1) call myself a slut, which I was not, so I wouldn't, or 2) get married, which also wasn't happening. Instead, I did the only thing I felt could do. I left.

As I walked out of the room, my father said, "Come back in here, Carmen. We aren't done." He didn't know how wrong he was.

I stormed off, slamming the door to my bedroom behind me and snatching up a spare duffel bag. I stuffed things inside the bag almost without looking. *My father would rather see me married at sixteen than accept that I am neither a bride nor a virgin. That matters more to him than my happiness or my future. Fine, then.* I'd figure out how to get along on my own.

As for my sister, I didn't know what I would do if I had to face her.

The man who would become my stalker was not really named Cory. I have not used his real name here, because I haven't spoken it since the last time I saw him. When I name something, I give it power, and he no longer has power over me.

I didn't run away from home to be with Cory but to escape my father, who could have come for me at any time. My father had chased after my sister to force her into a marriage, but he didn't come for me. Maybe he thought he should handle things different-ly this time. Maybe he knew I would never give in like my sister had. Or maybe he just gave up on me.

I escaped a tyrant and ended up in the hands of a bully. At first, Cory was kind to me. I never felt he was in love with me, but I thought he at least cared about me. Then he started hitting me. Soon he was beating me, or forcing me to the ground and stomping on me. "You're mine, Carmen," he would say. "We're together now." From another man, that might have sounded sweet. In his mouth, those words were a threat. *If I can't have you, no one will.*

Once, he stomped me so badly he broke my nose. I couldn't believe it. How could this be real? I had always been a fighter. Born defiant, I always drove my father crazy. But when a man hurts me physically, how could I fight back? I wasn't strong enough to put him in his place. I remember thinking, *This is the man my father wanted me to marry.*

Never for a moment did I think I deserved what Cory did to me. The problem was that, by then, I had nowhere else to go. For six terrible months, I kept in touch with only my mother. My father wouldn't speak to me and had forbidden my mother from helping me out. He seemed to think I'd gotten exactly what I deserved. Never did I believe that I *deserved what Cory did to me.*

My mother and I met every day after school—a small defiance, but my mother was not by nature a defiant woman. It meant a lot to know that she loved me enough to break my father's rules. Maybe it was the old guilt over the circumstances surrounding my birth, or perhaps it was all she felt she could do for me at that time. She couldn't fix things between my father and me, but she could keep track of me in case I ever changed my mind about coming home.

I stayed in school despite everything I was going through in my life. I didn't know how to get away from Cory, but I did know that I would eventually. I also knew that bigger things in my future would require a high school education.

One day, with winter coming on, I asked my mother a favor. "Can you bring one of my coats? I didn't think to pack any when I left." I had thought I'd be home by winter. I thought my father would have waved a white flag when he saw that I was serious.

My mother hesitated. "I don't know. Your father…" She trailed off. Yes, we both knew my father.

Fall was setting in, and the leaves were dying on the trees. "But it's getting cold," I said.

She sighed. "I'll think about it." Her eyes traced my face, lingering on my nose, which was beginning to heal. I wanted to tell her that she was trapped, too: even if my father didn't hit her, he was the one who called the shots. If my mother couldn't stand up to my father, then she definitely couldn't help me escape from Cory.

I walked back to my new home, my arms wrapped around myself to keep warm.

That night, Cory asked, "Are you thinking about leaving me, Carmen?"

I didn't say anything. How could I be thinking about anything else *but* escape?

"If you do," he told me, "I'll kill your parents."

"Leave my family out of this," I told him.

He leaned in close. "I don't *want* to hurt them. I want you to stay."

Damn, I was tired of being manipulated. My mother was not a fighter, but I knew I had to be. I wasn't going to let this man run my life or threaten my family.

One day, while walking home from my afternoon job, I noticed a familiar car on the road. My father sat in the driver's seat, and I could see the anger in his face as he recognized me. Before I could process what was happening, he'd swerved the car onto the sidewalk, leaped out, and grabbed my neck. He didn't say a word as he tossed me into his car.

It was only a short ride to my family's apartment, and I spent it practically paralyzed. Maybe I could have leaped out the car door, but I had no chance of escaping him on foot. Mostly, I was stunned. How could my own father turn on me like that? Wasn't he the one who was supposed to save me?

When we reached the house, he threw the car into park, grabbed me again, and dragged me up the stairs to our second-floor apartment and through the front door. My mother came out to meet him, and I watched her mouth fall open as he dragged me down the hall.

Finally my father let go of me. I thought the moment of my escape had come, but before I could move, I felt the flat of his hand on my face. "I'm ashamed of you," he shouted. . He hit me again.

I was vaguely aware of my mother's presence. She watched as he continued to hit me, but she said nothing. She came from a time when women considered a husband's word as law. The new law in my family was, "We are ashamed of Carmen."

*At least my father won't break my nose,* I thought bitterly.

Another blow landed, and when no more followed, I looked up. My father was panting as if he'd run a marathon. "I want you to leave now," he gasped.

A few months before, I would have asked him why he'd dragged me home just to ask me to leave again. Instead, I simply stormed out, pushing past my still-silent mother on my way. Every time I got away from someone who wanted to dictate my life to me, I ran into someone else who wanted to do the same thing.

The next time I saw my mother, she didn't say a word about what had happened with my father. She did bring me a coat, though.

I quietly plotted my getaway from Cory. I would do whatever I could to evade him. He was getting more and more jealous and paranoid, and he increased his violence against me. When any other guy so much as looked at me, Cory would threaten him. He was a *Dateline* episode in the making. "That guy wants to steal you," he said, as if I were a wallet or luxury car.

Whenever he felt insecure or worried that he was losing control, he took it out on me. In the middle of one of these beatings, I fought back. Furious, he pulled me up and slammed my head into the wall. When I tried to get away, he slammed my head against a window so hard the glass shattered. As glassy shards rained down around me, I finally understood that this man would not stop until I was dead.

Shocked by the destruction, he let his grip on me slip. I pulled away. When he reached for me again, I stood my ground. "You're a coward," I told him.

"If you leave me—" he began, reaching for another threat.

"Of course I'm leaving you!" I snarled. Maybe it was my anger that stopped him in his tracks. Maybe I was so cut up by the glass that I actually frightened him. Whatever the reason, he didn't try to stop me this time. Turning my back on my father in the months before had been an act of defiance and pride. Turning my back on Cory was more than that. My life needed saving, and nobody else was coming to the rescue.

So I saved myself. Once again, I left.

After leaving Cory, I lived a few weeks with friends and their families. I got another job and saved everything I could so that someday soon I could get my own apartment. Sometimes I felt like an airplane circling overhead, looking for a safe place to land. Throughout all this my family always knew where to find me, but I was glad my dad hadn't shown up at a friend's house to take his anger out on me again.

I still met my mother after school daily. "You could come home," she suggested one day.

"Come home and live with him? You're kidding."

"It wouldn't kill you to swallow your pride," she said.

She was right. I'd gotten away from a guy who really might have killed me. Unfortunately, Cory kept following me around. He was sure to find me wherever I was. "Cory threatened to kill you," I told her. "I can't get rid of him."

"Your father's tough," my mother said. That was true. My father might not have come to save me, but if I went home and begged his forgiveness, I knew he would be able to keep me safe while I was at home. I wasn't sure he'd do it out of love, but he had his pride, too. He wouldn't let me get hurt while I was under his protection.

I wanted freedom but didn't yet know how to get it. I knew that if I saved my paychecks and kept up with school, I would be better able to make good choices about my living situation. In the meantime, I needed to live somewhere relatively safe.

I settled for the lesser of the two evils. I moved back in with my parents. The atmosphere in our apartment was tense, and nobody was really happy with the arrangement, but my father kept his behavior in check.

I often saw Cory hanging around in the street outside our apartment. Sometimes he threatened our visitors. He was a shadow I couldn't shake, but I had a plan. After I graduated from high school, I would take courses and work whatever jobs I could find. I would manage my problems until I found a way to solve them. *After all*, I thought, *nobody's going to solve them for me.*

That was one reason I fell so quickly for Tony. He became my hero on our first date, or at least my champion. With him, I didn't have to settle for the lesser evil or make excuses for how he treated me. He treated me with respect. That was all I'd ever asked for, really. Still, I needed a way to get rid of my stalker for good.

# CHAPTER FOUR

I t didn't take very long for me to realize I really liked Tony and that I wanted to keep him in my life. He was a gentleman. I'd never dated a gentleman before. Still, I worried. I was never afraid Tony would hurt me physically. One good thing that came from dating Cory was that I'd learned what to watch for when it came to picking boyfriends.

Instead, I worried that he'd hurt me by leaving. I'd never met anyone like him and was sure I never would again.

A few other people had left, although none of them mattered to me as much as Tony did. Cory had run them off, one by one, in an attempt to isolate me. Maybe he thought he could get me back or maybe he just wanted me to be unhappy; either way, he did his best to make sure I was alone.

A few months before I met Tony, my brother Richie had set me up with his friend. I didn't know the guy, but Richie promised me we'd get along and that this friend was nothing like Cory. The friend came to pick me up for our date. I saw him leave his car and walk toward my building. A few steps from my door, Cory intercepted him.

I don't know how Cory found out about that date. I don't know what Cory said to my brother's friend. All I know is that, after a brief conversation, my date turned and ran for his car. Richie apologized later on behalf of the guy who'd stood me up. I shook my head. "He can't protect me. I don't want a boyfriend like that."

It was nice to know that I hadn't missed out on much. I'd dated one coward already and didn't need another one in my life. Still, it would have been nice to decide that for myself.

Cory had decided that if he couldn't have me, no one would. I'd gotten away before he could do any of the worst things he'd threatened me with, so he'd found another way to have me to himself.

I prayed that it wouldn't be the same with Tony.

Tony and I had only gone out a few times when my worst fear came to fruition. Tony dropped me off after our date, and I noticed Cory hanging around the apartment building. I sank lower in my seat, hoping he wouldn't see us.

"What's wrong?" Tony asked me.

"That's him," I hissed.

Tony turned and eyed my stalker. "Huh," was all he said.

Cory, his hands balled into fists, stormed at the car. My window was open, so he reached in and tried to drag me out onto the street.

Tony swore and pulled me back in. I cranked the window up as fast as I could—we didn't have the luxury of power windows, which would have been a lifesaver.

"Get out!" yelled Cory as he banged on the car door.

I cringed. Not only was I afraid of what Cory would do if he got his hands on me, but I was also convinced that Tony would decide he didn't need this in his life. I was sure he wasn't a coward, but he'd be crazy to want to deal with this after every date we went on. Cory hovered around the car, shouting and making threatening gestures through the window.

"What are we going to do?" I asked.

Tony stared out the window. He didn't look frightened. He seemed to be sizing Cory up, and I wondered what he saw. "Get out of the car," Tony said at last, calmly.

I felt bitter disappointment. *Wow*, I wanted to tell him. *I thought you were different. I thought you would protect me, but you're just like everyone else, telling me to get out.* I reached for the handle and was surprised when Tony stepped out and came around the car to stand by my door as I emerged.

"You'd better stay away from my girl," Cory said.

Tony eyed him up and down, clearly unimpressed. "Are you sure she's your girl?"

I hovered by the car, keeping Tony standing between me and the man who had harassed me for the last two and a half years. "That's funny," Tony said. He stared Cory down, always keeping himself between us. "What's she doing in another man's car?"

Cory paused, as taken aback by Tony's attitude as I was. He'd obviously expected Tony to run like all the other guys had, but he was wrong.

"Go inside, Carmen," Tony said.

Cory might not have known what to do, but I did. I became an Olympic runner, I flew through the air, ducked into the apartment hallway, and didn't stop until I burst through the apartment door, slamming it behind me. My mother came from the kitchen, eyebrows raised. I leaned against the front door, panting with relief.

"Are you OK?" she asked.

I nodded before sprinting to my room, where my window looked out into the street. Tony waited on the sidewalk below, hands in his pockets. "That guy's on his way up to kill you," Tony informed me.

"Is he?" I asked.

Tony shrugged. "That's what he says." It had occurred to me before that Cory might kill me, but the way Tony said it made me laugh. I had backup this time, and my backup wasn't scared.

A few seconds later, I heard pounding on the front door of the apartment. I assumed my parents wouldn't let him in.

I was wrong. After a few knocks, I heard the door open. "I'm here to see Carmen." His voice, even muffled through the walls, still made my skin crawl.

After a pause, my father called, "Carmen, someone's here to see you!" He knew Cory, of course, and should have known not to let him in.

"Lock the door!" I hollered. "I don't want to deal with him!"

From the street below, I could hear Tony chuckling.

I heard shuffling in our living room. At last my father said, "She doesn't want to see you." If my mother had answered the door, Cory likely would have forced his way through or held her hostage until I'd come out to see him. He didn't argue with my father, however. He just left.

It had never occurred to me before, but Tony saw the truth about my stalker. Cory could rough up a woman but was too scared to fight a man. He would fight only if he was sure to win. He really was a coward. I'd known that for a long time, but I also knew what he was capable of. When he felt in charge, he was dangerous. I just hadn't known how to take his control away.

Thank God for Tony. When Cory tried to leave the apartment building, Tony blocked his way. I watched from the window, keeping my face out of sight but curious to see what happened. "So," Tony asked, "did you do it? Did you kill her?"

Cory hurried away, disappearing around the corner.

Tony waved good-bye to me and strolled back to his car, shaking his head. My heart had never felt so light.

I thought Cory might leave me alone after that, but it was not to be. Tony proved my stalker to be a coward, but even a coward has his pride.

The next day as I was leaving for my job at a radiology office downtown, I stepped into the stairwell, only to have Cory grab me and shove me against a wall. He punched me in the face twice. If not for the burst of pain that accompanied each blow, I'd have thought I was having a nightmare.

I twisted away from him and dashed back to the apartment. Neither of us said a word. Cory didn't have to say anything. As I slammed the door behind me, I finally admitted to myself that as long as my ex was in the picture, I would never feel safe leaving my apartment. That was his point, surely. No matter what, Cory would find a way to intimidate me.

I went into the kitchen, where for once I had the room to myself. I was shaking from shock and adrenaline, my fingers trembling on the phone's buttons. While it rang, I twisted my finger through the spiral cord, trying to calm myself with the simple repetitive motion.

I wasn't calm. "Hello?" I almost burst into tears at the sound of Tony's voice. I generally wasn't a crier, but I could already feel my face becoming bruised.

I was going to be late to work, and I wished I could find a way to put the situation behind me. Cory's constant harassment had worn me down. "Tony?" I choked out. "It's Carmen."

"What's wrong?" Tony demanded. "Is it that guy again?"

"He attacked me in the hallway." I swallowed, breathing slowly to calm the panic in my voice. "He might still be out there. I don't know. I have to get to work."

"I'm coming," said Tony. "Stay right there."

"What are you going to do?" I asked.

"I'm taking you to work," he said. "I'll take you to the store. I'm going to take you wherever you need to go until this guy backs off."

I didn't know what to say. I'd called just to hear his voice, not to make him dash out to my rescue. "This sounds an awful lot like taking care of me," I said at last.

"That again? Carmen, if you want me to buy you shoes or jewelry or a car, I'll tell you to take care of yourself. This isn't the same thing. Let me help you."

I paused and then told him, "OK, I'll wait."

Tony took me to work that day and for the next few days after that. At first I was anxious every time we left the apartment. Tony stuck with me, and soon

I stopped feeling nervous and felt genuinely safe for the first time in years.

Cory never bothered me again. I heard later that he'd gone to jail for stabbing someone. I wasn't surprised. It was all too easy to imagine myself at the other end of his knife. He'd cut me when we were dating: just one of the many things he'd done to make me feel helpless and small.

I was never helpless. I stood up to him and fought for my life. Without Tony, though, I'm not sure I could have won.

Tony saved me. Later, it would be my job to return the favor.

# CHAPTER FIVE

Tony sent me a letter after we started dating in which he remembered the moment we first clicked:

*I'm your missing other half (for real) Carmen. It's like the first time we went out when I came to get you, and you had the same outfit on as I did, and from that day you've been on my f---ing nerves ever since. Me and you. That's what it's all about, together forever, can you dig it, I can, it's in my heart for real.*

Three months after Tony and I met, we moved in together. It must have seemed hasty to my family, especially after everything I'd been through at the hands of another man, but Tony was right in that letter he wrote. From the moment we saw each other in our matching Levi's suits, we both knew we'd found someone special. I'd been missing him in my life but hadn't known it until we met.

When my father told me to marry Cory, I'd been positive that marrying him wasn't what I wanted. With Tony, I felt just the opposite.

"You're rushing into this, Carmen," my mother warned me.

Tony and I were living only a few blocks away. "I know," I told her, "but he's the one, Ma."

"Are you going to marry him?" She looked at me from the corner of her eye while stirring beans over the stove. I missed that familiar smell in my new apartment, but I didn't miss having to eat them.

"I am."

"When?"

I shrugged. "When we're ready."

"Hmm." My mother paused. "You're getting married in a Catholic church, of course?"

I swallowed. Tony's family was Baptist. I couldn't tell my mother that his family wanted us to get married in a Baptist church. She'd have died right in front of the stove. "Of course," I said. "A Catholic wedding. Absolutely."

Tony and I were not married yet, but I was determined to make our home look welcoming. We lived on a busy street in a small, rundown apartment. I was a receptionist in a radiology lab, and I hoped to turn that into a career once I could afford to take more classes. Tony worked as a barber. He was great at what he did, but it wasn't a job that made him rich.

None of us in that neighborhood had much money, but I didn't see why we shouldn't come home to a comfortable apartment. I got nice furniture for our new place so our living room wouldn't be cluttered with mismatched pieces. I kept my plan secret from Tony, thinking it would be a nice surprise for him to come home one day to find our worn-out living room transformed into a chic lounge.

I went to a nearby store and picked out a set of white wicker furniture. I was pleased with myself for having found the set. I liked the look of it, and it didn't cost too much. When the delivery truck arrived, the two men who unloaded everything seemed a little confused, but neither of them said anything to me. I spent the afternoon arranging everything until I thought the place looked very tidy and homey.

When Tony came home that evening, I sat in the living room on our new love seat, feeling pretty smug for coming up with such a nice surprise. Tony stepped into the living room and stopped cold. He looked at me, looked at the furniture, and laughed. I chuckled to myself, but Tony didn't stop laughing. Every time he looked up, he laughed harder.

I felt a little annoyed. "What's with you?" I asked at last.

"Where did you find this stuff?"

I sat up a little straighter. "The place around the corner. Don't you like it?"

"Carmen," he said, "you found the only place in Harlem that had patio furniture for sale."

It had not even occurred to me, but Tony was right. My white wicker chairs, love seat, and coffee table were meant for outdoor use. I was furious with the salesman for letting me make a fool of myself. "Who has a patio in Harlem?"

"Not us," said Tony. "That's for sure."

"Well, I like it," I said, partly to salvage my pride and partly because we really needed furniture and I'd already paid for it.

Tony wiped his eyes, still grinning. "If you like it, I like it," he said.

We kept that furniture for years. In the end we were glad to have it, but Tony never did let me live it down.

Our Harlem apartment was not what I was used to. Although we were close to my family's place, two blocks made a lot of difference in the vibes of the neighborhoods. The sidewalks at our new place were always crowded with pimps and prostitutes. The women in particular were like nobody I'd ever met: they wore bright clothes that showed off their bodies and talked directly about their sexuality with complete strangers. At first I was horrified. My mother would have had a few words to say about them if she'd known.

When I brought this up with Tony, he shook his head. "They aren't bad people," he said. "They look out for each other. They'll look out for us, too."

It was true. Despite the roughness of the neighborhood, our car was never once vandalized. The pimps and prostitutes on the street made sure of it, since everyone liked Tony. He stayed out of their business, but he always treated that crowd with respect, which was more than their clients often did. Soon they were looking after me as well and making sure people left me alone.

As a kid, I hadn't known that places like our new neighborhood existed anywhere in the world, much less two blocks from our front door. My father took care of my mother and the kids, even if I didn't like his methods. I was used to some semblance of sanity and stability; up until Cory, my life had been mostly safe and cloistered.

Tony's world was different from the world I'd known. He liked to go to the kinds of parties and clubs where my modest dress would get me turned away at the door if I hadn't been on Tony's arm.

Hip-hop was making its appearance in Harlem. All around our neighborhood, men sported heavy gold chains. Tony was no exception. I wondered later what we'd have done with the money if he hadn't spent it on all that gold jewelry, but it made him happy, so I didn't complain.

In those days, Tony cut the hair of a lot of celebrities. The boxer Mike Tyson was a regular, along with a number of rappers and musicians. I was amazed by Tony's world, and I was always ready to go out and have a good time, even if I refused to wear the skimpy clothes a lot of places demanded. Tony didn't ask me to change that. The two of us worked during the day and then went out late into the night to enjoy the ever-changing beats of the clubs.

As a high schooler, I'd longed to be part of the cool crowd. Now, Tony *was* the cool crowd, and he never asked me to change who I was. I did change, except that this time I didn't do it to make anyone else happy. I changed because I was happy to be the best I could be.

One morning I woke to find Tony watching me with a funny smile on his face. "Hey, Carmen," he said. "I've been thinking."

I yawned. "About what?"

"Thinking we should get married."

"Of course we should," I said. "We talked about this. We just have to figure out how to make both our mothers happy and—"

"I think we should get married today."

I sat up. "Like, now?"

"Why not?" Tony was smiling, but he was obviously serious.

I looked at the clock. "I have work in a few hours."

"I can drop you off afterward."

"I…"

Tony waited, not rushing me, not backpedaling. I couldn't imagine my mother's reaction if I were to get married behind her back without a ceremony or priest or dress or vows or any Catholic rituals. My father's response would be more predictable—he wouldn't be happy. But the idea of being Tony's wife by the time we fell asleep that night, without having the pressure of planning a wedding, was too appealing to pass up.

"OK," I said at last. "But let me get dressed first." Tony grinned at me and leaned over for a kiss.

I dressed for work, since I wouldn't have time to change. We would just do it in the courthouse rather than in a church. Tony dressed in a black zip-up jogging suit and yellow sweatshirt. Before we left, he pulled on a Steelers cap. "Well," I observed, "at least you match."

He walked to the car, pulling keys from the pocket of his tracksuit as he went, but I stopped short. "There won't be any parking by the courthouse. We should take the train."

"Carmen, we've talked about this." Tony jingled the keys. "We can find parking."

"There's nothing wrong with the train."

He held his ground. "The whole subway system is full of crazy people. We have a car. Let's take the car."

I crossed my arms and shook my head, but in the end I got in the car. When we reached the courthouse, we found an empty spot right across the street. Tony gave me a smug look. "See?" he said. "All that grief you gave me, and there's a parking space right here."

I admitted my defeat, and the two of us walked up to the courthouse, grinning like fools. A woman in the lobby flipped through a magazine; she appeared to be waiting for someone. We were the only other people there, besides the staff.

The clerk gave us paperwork to fill out and asked us for identification. "This all looks good to me," he said. "Where's your witness?"

"Witness?" I repeated blankly.

"You need a witness to be married," explained the clerk, as if that should have been obvious. I turned to Tony, who just shrugged.

The woman waiting in the lobby looked up from her magazine. "I can be your witness," she offered, "unless you've got someone else."

No way was I calling my mother to witness my courthouse marriage. "We'd appreciate it," I told the woman.

It was a strange wedding. It wasn't at all what my mother would have chosen for me, but it felt right. If we'd been married in a Catholic church, then we would have sworn our vows: "For richer, for poorer, in sickness and in health, until death do us part." I didn't need to say those words while wearing a white dress in front of a roomful of witnesses for them to be true. I felt it, and I know Tony felt it. That was enough for me.

We thanked our volunteer witness for her time and headed back out to the street to find a yellow parking ticket shoved beneath the windshield wipers of the car. Our too-good-to-be-true parking space wasn't a valid space after all. I rounded on Tony at once. "I told you!" I cried. "We should have taken the train!"

Tony laughed and pulled me in for a kiss. "I'll drive you to work," he assured me, "and pay the ticket after."

Just this once, I let it go.

In those days I was always late to work, but it was usually only a few minutes. Everyone at that job knew I worked hard enough during my shift to make up for it, so for the most part nobody said anything. They knew I was in love and bound to be a little scattered. The day we got married, however, I was noticeably late.

One manager waved to me when I came in but said nothing. The other stomped over and scowled. "Why are you late this time?" he demanded.

My coworkers watched intently all around me. I'm sure they were prepared for a public shaming, and possibly even a firing. The words burst out of me much louder than I intended. "I got married!"

My manager's frown transformed in an instant. "Congratulations!" he said. "Why didn't you say anything? We'll throw you a bridal shower, of course!"

They were all thrilled. I could think of someone who might not be thrilled, though. When I got home that night, I dropped my purse onto the wicker love seat next to Tony and stood paralyzed by a thought I had somehow avoided until then. Tony looked up at me. "Something wrong?" he asked.

"What on earth am I going to tell my mother?"

"I don't know," Tony said. "I love you, but that's something you'll have to do on your own. It would be wise to tell her soon, though, or you'll have to admit that you kept it a secret."

The two-block walk to my family's apartment felt like I'd walked for miles. I imagined I was marching toward my execution. The climb up the stairs to the second floor exhausted me. By the time I knocked on the door, my legs felt like lead. My mother invited me into her kitchen. She examined my face but didn't say a word. "Ma," I began, "I...I married Tony today."

"*Ay, Dios mio!*" she exclaimed.

"We went to the courthouse and signed all the paperwork. It's done." I tried to keep my voice light, and a little bit of the happiness I'd felt all day pushed through my fear of how my mother would react.

She bent her head and clasped her hands in front of her. It felt like I'd sat there for days as my mother said the Hail Mary and Our Father over and over, fifty times, a hundred times, to beg the Lord for my forgiveness and salvation. She suddenly sat up and brushed away the tears. "Congratulations, Carmen," she said at last. "I'm very happy for you."

I knew the news of my non-Catholic marriage nearly broke her heart, but she meant what she said. She was happy that I was happy, and if that was all I could get, then I'd take it.

# CHAPTER SIX

There are things in life we are taught to never talk about. We keep our silence because we are afraid of being heard. We forget because we don't want to remember. It's easier to pack our memories away and pretend that things didn't happen than to act.

With Tony on my side, it was easier for me to face the memories I'd kept to myself for a long time. I trusted him to listen without pitying me. I never wanted pity. All I wanted was someone to share my history with. I wanted him to know everything about me and to love me anyway.

The first secret I told Tony was about my brother. My oldest brother was ten years older than me. I wasn't nearly as close with him as I was with Richie, mainly because of his age but also because he seemed to have so many secrets.

When I was six years old, my brother found me playing a game by myself in the family room. He watched me for a while without saying anything, and I ignored him. My brother thought he was too cool to play games with me, so I didn't even bother to ask. "Carmen," he said at last, "Will you come with me for a minute?"

I looked up. "What for?"

"It's a surprise." He gestured for me to follow.

I went with him down the hall to the boys' room. Richie and my middle brother weren't around, so it was just the two of us. The boys usually slammed the door in my face and told me to keep out, but my brother opened the door and waited. I hovered by the door, used to being shut out rather than invited in. When I hesitated, he said, "I've got something to show you."

I went into the boys' room, and my brother closed the door behind me. I could tell something strange was going on, but I wasn't sure what it might be. Whatever he had to show me, he obviously didn't want anybody else to see. He sat down on the bed. "Come here," he said. I went to sit beside him. "No," he said, "here." He sat me on his lap.

He was nearly as tall as my father by then: almost a grown-up. I didn't sit on my father's lap very often. Despite their similarities in height, something was very different about this experience. My brother wriggled beneath me, breathing hard, and I suddenly felt very uncomfortable.

I trusted my brother. He was family, and that meant we were supposed to look out for each other. "Now put your hands here," he said, pulling my hands toward his lap and showing me how he wanted me to touch him. "Yeah, like that."

Something was very wrong. I felt guilty for being part of it and then ashamed of my guilt. I couldn't have said at the time what exactly was wrong, but it wasn't the sort of thing I knew how to talk about with my mother. Nobody had told me about sex or anything like it, but I knew the rules any preschooler was taught: *Don't touch yourself. Keep your clothes on when you're around others. Don't invade other people's personal space.*

My brother knew the rules, too. When he unzipped his pants and told me where and how to touch him, I had to fight back tears. My brother then told me I could leave, and I ran to my room.

"What's with you?" my sister asked.

I had nothing to say. Nobody had given me the words to explain what our brother had done to me.

I avoided my brother for a long time after that. If anyone in our family noticed that I ducked out of the room when he came in or avoided looking at him over the dinner table, they didn't say so.

Now I know how often this happens. It was my brother in my case, but for someone else it could be a cousin, an uncle, a father. I kept my mouth closed because I felt as if I'd done something wrong, and telling someone what had happened would feel the same as admitting guilt. I had participated in a shameful act that I didn't fully understand. In the Bible stories we were taught at our Catholic church, people were punished for their sins. I asked myself, *Am I a sinner?* I didn't know.

My brother never invited me into his room again, and I tried to forget he'd ever asked me to touch him. I crushed the memory to the point where I'd never have to confront it.

Tony was the first person I ever told, but he wouldn't be the last. My brother left me alone after that, but if I had told someone what had happened that day, I might have saved the people I loved a lot of heartbreak.

I only ever shared the second secret with Tony. At my high school was one very good-looking boy all the girls crushed on. Jon was the hottest boy in school, and everybody knew it, himself included. In the lunchroom, girls watched him walk by and giggled to one another.

He and I never talked, but we did have a few classes together. Jon ran with the cool crowd. I did not. He was pretty to look at, but I had no reason to think he'd ever notice me.

One day after school, Jon came up to me in the schoolyard. "Hey, Carmen," he said.

I was so surprised Jon knew my name that I assumed he wasn't talking to me. But he'd said my name.

I glanced around to see if perhaps he was talking to another girl named Carmen. A group of girls lounging on the steps watched us from the corners of their eyes. I'm sure they were checking Jon out and wondering what he was doing with me. I wondered the same thing.

"I want to ask you about a homework problem from math class," he said. "We're in the same period."

My mouth suddenly went dry. He really was talking to me. I knew we were in the same period; what surprised me was that he knew, too.

"Could you explain it to me?" he asked.

"Sure," I said at last. "I'll see if I can help."

Jon turned his head to examine the other girls, who seemed to be ignoring us. A few other people were hanging around the school, waiting for their parents or chatting with their friends before they split up to walk home. "Let's go somewhere else," he suggested.

"Yeah," I said. "We can look over the book and go through it step by step."

School was always important to me, and I was flattered that Jon had noticed how well I did in class. He could have asked anyone for help, and any girl would have been glad to do him a favor, but he chose me.

He led me between the side of the school and a wall that cut the school off from the rest of the neighborhood. We weren't really off school property, but the place was out of sight. Anyone who was standing outside the school would be at the wrong angle to see us, and nobody else had any reason to be back there. It was a private place where we could study without interruption. "Back here," Jon said, pointing. I followed him behind the building.

He turned to me. I didn't realize how close we were until he reached for my hand. "You're really pretty, Carmen," he said. "Do you know that?"

"I'm not sure—" I began, but he cut me off with a kiss. It occurred to me then that every girl in the school yard would be jealous of what was happening to me, but I only felt confused. We'd never even talked before. Jon was kissing me, which I guessed was a good thing, but I wasn't really sure why he was doing it.

My confusion soon turned to fright. Jon pushed me back toward the wall, still kissing me. I tried to pull away, but he wouldn't let me go. His hands were all over me, grabbing me, pulling at my clothes. My panty hose ripped when he yanked at them, and I cursed myself for wearing a skirt instead of jeans. I tried to push him away, but he caught me off balance and crushed himself against me. His fingers, groping under my skirt, found the line of my panties.

I was naive, but I understood what Jon wanted, and I wasn't prepared to let him have it. I pushed back, hitting him wherever I could reach. The harder he held me, the harder I fought.

I'm not sure why he let me go. Maybe he was afraid someone would hear us and come to investigate. Maybe he realized I was serious about wanting to get away.

What I do know is that his grip on me let up, and before he could change his mind, I ran for it.

As soon as I was in sight of other people, I slowed my run to a jog and then a walk. My heart still pounding, I did my best to slow my breathing. When I was sure no one was looking, I adjusted my skirt to hide the tear in my panty hose. I didn't want anyone to know what had happened.

I knew I was lucky to get away from Jon, but I also blamed myself for letting anything happen in the first place. *Was it my fault for following him? For failing to fight him off faster? For doing whatever it was that had attracted his attention in the first place?*

It was a relief to tell Tony about it, even years later. I'd remained silent because I was afraid of what people might think of me. Now when I tell my story, I feel less alone. If I had spoken to someone at the time, then Jon might have gotten in trouble. It might have discouraged him from attacking another girl. Someone might have told me that it wasn't my fault that I'd followed him. It was Jon's fault—just as it had been my brother's fault before that—for betraying my trust.

When I told Tony, he put his arms around me. There was nothing he could do to fix what had happened, so he didn't try. Instead, he gave me the chance to trust him. After what had happened with my brother, my father, Jon, and Cory, I could have become bitter. I could have sworn off men. People tend to give up on love, and love is the one thing I will never give up on.

Everything I had been through was worth it, because in the end I found Tony. I was determined to keep him. Other men had noticed me before, but for the first time, I was in love with someone who truly loved me back.

# CHAPTER SEVEN

Tony and I hadn't spent a lot of time around each other's families until we got married. I hoped my family would love him as much as I did. I hoped they'd at least accept him. That wasn't the case at first, though, mostly because of my father. Maybe he found Tony's easy confidence off-putting, but most likely the color of Tony's skin challenged my father to accept him as a son-in-law.

When I was a kid, my father never had nice things to say about people with skin darker than his own. If we passed a black person on the street, my father would mutter "Monkeys" under his breath. He was Puerto Rican, as was my mother; he always felt that the lighter your skin, the more respect you deserved. He was a relatively pale Latino, and he took great pride in that.

My mother was darker than him. My father felt that her role in the family should be different because of this. Sometimes he sent her to his mother's house (my grandmother's) to do the cleaning. His mother, after all, had lighter skin than my mother did and was therefore better than her. Occasionally, at my father's request, my mother cleaned the homes of other family members. I don't recall her ever complaining about it. I don't know if she felt this was her lot as a darker-skinned woman or if she just felt she should obey her husband.

My father was old-fashioned, stuck in a world he'd left behind when he and my mother moved to New York. Imagine how my father felt when I married a black man. I didn't fall in love with Tony just to annoy my father, but is it any surprise that all his children were engaged or married to black people at some point in their lives?

Fortunately, my father long ago gave up on the idea that I would ever do what he told me to do. Once my mother had accepted the news of my marriage, my father kept his thoughts more or less to himself. He was a little cool toward his black son-in-law, but I didn't expect him to back me up all at once. Some people see others in terms of being black, white, Latino, Asian, and so on, but it's also possible to be racist against members of one's own race. If I'd married a dark-skinned Latino, then he would have thought I'd married down. Never mind that I'd married a black man.

Tony's family wasn't sure what to make of me, either. At one family gathering, Tony overheard an aunt say, "We always knew he was different. Look at what he married!"

Tony turned to her to say something in my defense, but his mother beat him to it. "If Tony wants to be married to a foreigner, that's his business." When Tony told me about it later, he laughed at that line.

"If they think Puerto Rico is foreign," I told him, "they don't know their history!"

"Forget about it." Tony kissed me. "They like you. They'll get over it."

In any case, we were ready to make our own family. Our parents were unsettled by us, but we were happy. They'd have to get used to it.

Tony had a daughter, Tracie, whom he had told me about the night we met. She  lived with her mother. Whenever we had a chance to see her, we showered her with an outpouring of love and affection. I got the feeling she wanted to spend more time with her father and that she'd open up once she knew me better. But her mother didn't like either of us very much. We knew that she didn't want Tracie to get too comfortable with us, so she never really did.

When I gave birth to my daughter, Ellie, I was pleased she was a girl. Girls could be trouble—I knew that very well—but at least I had firsthand experience in that department.

Tony and I stopped going to parties and clubs to focus on the house and our jobs. We saved what we could, because we knew how expensive kids were. I'd seen how hard the five of us had been on my mother. We were more work than a full-time job would have been. She'd made a lot of sacrifices for us, and while I was grateful for this, I wanted more out of life than only being a mom. I told myself that Ellie would be my only baby. I'd have the best of both worlds. I could be a mother and have my own life, too.

When I held my daughter for the first time, I felt as if I could see her whole life stretching out before her. She would be an only child, and Tony and I would provide her with everything she needed. She'd go to school and choose a career she loved; once she had that, she could start a family of her own.

I loved my family. I was not nearly as passionate about my job at the radiology lab. It was good work that paid well, but it didn't move me. I sometimes wished I'd waited a little longer to start a family so that I could have found a career I loved as much as I loved my husband and baby girl. I promised Ellie she'd have a chance to do something that fulfilled her. Tony and I would do what we could to give her the best possible future.

Ellie was my first. She was a gift. I loved her more than I could have imagined. Tony and I made sure she had everything we could give her from the day she was born. She was my special child. I knew she'd be a little like Tony and a little like me, but mostly something of her own. I wanted her to be safe forever and to never want for anything.

Ellie was all I ever wanted, the only child I needed. She was perfect.

"When are we going to try again?" asked Tony.

I was holding Ellie. She had just fallen asleep, and I was smiling to myself, feeling pretty content with this new turn my life had taken. "Try what again?"

Tony gave me a funny look. "When are we going to try for a boy?"

I hoped to see a joking smile on his face but wasn't so lucky. "We aren't," I said. "One is plenty."

Tony frowned, which was the first clue I had that a storm was coming.

"Kids are trouble," I told him. Ellie wriggled in my arms. "Little kids, little problems. Big kids, big problems. You'll see. She'll be a handful."

"You've got a daughter," said Tony. "I want a son."

"We've got a daughter," I corrected him.

"A girl for you, a boy for me." Tony crossed his arms.

"Forget it," I said. "I'm telling you, one's enough."

Tony closed his eyes. "We'll talk about it later." He got up from the white wicker chair that had become his usual spot in the living room.

"There's nothing to talk about," I insisted.

He didn't answer, and my voice woke Ellie, who started crying. By the time I'd calmed her, I'd already halfway forgotten the conversation. I knew how to be stubborn. I'd dig my heels in and hold my ground, and eventually Tony would see sense.

Except that he didn't. A second baby, the son Tony wanted, became the topic of almost every conversation we had. Tony wanted a boy. I wanted to have time for my work, my interests. I was afraid of becoming my mother. Running the house was her life's work, but even she had wanted to stop at three. Look how that turned out.

Lying in bed beside my husband, both of us too angry to sleep, I could empathize with my mother more than ever. For the first time, I really understood how she must have felt when she hadn't been able to choose how many of us there would be. Thinking about her situation only made me more stubborn. No one could force me to have kids I didn't want. Not even Tony.

One day, when Ellie was almost three, I came home from work to find a pile of bags beside the door. I stepped around them and made my way to the bedroom, where I found my husband angrily packing his clothes into a duffel bag.

"What are you doing?" I demanded, but I already knew. I'd made a similar scene when my dad had tried to make me get married years before. Tony was running away. "Tony," I said, "put that down."

"Forget it," he snapped. "You made your decision. I've made mine. I can't stay with a woman who doesn't want to give me a son."

All that time, I'd thought it was a matter of holding my ground. Tony had allowed me to make my own decisions ever since we'd started dating, so I assumed he'd let me win if I fought hard enough and long enough. Looking at all his things packed up, I felt both defeated and afraid. I pictured what it would be like to come home to the empty apartment, what it would be like to raise Ellie on my own, how it would feel not just to be lonely, but to be lonely for *him*. How badly did I really want to win this fight?

Tony kept shoving his things into the bag, and I made my decision. "One," I said.

He paused. "One?"

"One more baby," I said, folding my arms and trying to sound like a negotiator and not a woman terrified she might actually lose her husband. "I don't know if it will be a boy or a girl, but we can try one more time. But that's it."

Tony turned to look at me as if he were measuring me up. Maybe he thought he should hold out for a better offer, try to get me to promise we could have however many children it took for us to have a boy, but there was no way I would agree to that.

"One," he repeated at last. "All right. That's fair."

I helped him unpack, relieved to have made that agreement. It seemed I'd lost the battle. Then again, I'd come awfully close to losing something that mattered a lot more to me.

I was pregnant within weeks of our agreement. When I found out, I let my hands lie on my belly and prayed: Please be a boy, please be a boy.

I could love another girl, but I wasn't sure what it would mean for my marriage. What if I had a second girl and Tony left anyway? If he were to pack his bags, would I crumble and agree to try yet again? *Carmen*, I thought, *you are some kind of fool.*

Tony was the one who wanted another baby, but if things went wrong, then I'd have no one but myself to blame. I went to my ultrasound alone. I wanted to be the one to tell Tony either way, and I didn't want him to see the look on my face when I found out whether our baby was a boy or a girl. Ellie stayed with my mother, and I kissed her before I left.

I rode the train to my appointment. A few passengers nodded at me and smiled, congratulating me. *Save that for the ride home!* I thought, which was uncharitable of me. I hugged my belly and resolved to love this baby no matter what happened.

By the time I reached the doctor's office, I was shaky and wound up. As the technician spread cool gel across my growing belly, I whispered under my breath, *Please, please, please.*

"Do you see him?" the nurse asked, pointing at the screen. "There's his head, his hands. Your son looks perfectly healthy."

Healthy was good, but the word *son* sent the air whooshing from my lungs. For the first time since I'd agreed to a second baby, I allowed myself to be happy about it. On the train ride home, I was practically floating despite my growing belly. When I danced into the apartment, Tony looked up in surprise. He must have seen the news on my face, because he got up and looked me in the eyes. "Is it…"

I nodded before the words had even left his mouth. My husband was a tough man. I'd seen him angry and defensive, but I'd never seen him cry. When I told him that he'd have a son, he dropped to his knees right there and kissed my stomach while tears poured down his cheeks. I'd never seen him so soft before.

I hadn't understood why a son mattered so much to him, but I finally realized how much he wanted a boy. I was glad I had relented just this once. Of course we named the baby Tony after his father.

My husband was ecstatic when Little Tony was born. And as hard as I'd fought against having him, I loved my son. Still, I kept thinking of my mother and how she'd tried to stop having kids. I had no doubt that if I gave Tony another couple of months to think about it, he'd want a third baby, and there was no way I would agree to that. If I were going to win that argument, I'd have to plan ahead.

My mother had tried to get her tubes tied. I decided that I would do the same—only I'd make sure they did it right. I went in for an exam and made the appointment, not breathing a word to Tony.

I told my friend Marcia what I was planning. "Aren't you worried he'll leave you?" she asked.

I considered this. "Maybe."

"And you're still going through with it?" She was clearly appalled.

"If he's going to leave, he'd better do it while we have only two kids for me to take care of," I told her. It sounded cold, but that was the truth. I knew other women who'd had babies to keep their husbands from leaving, but their husbands had left anyway. Besides, as much as I loved Tony, I wouldn't let him control my life.

On the day before the surgery, I stopped Tony as he was on his way to work. "I need you to drive me somewhere tomorrow," I told him. "I can probably take the train in, but I'll need you to pick me up."

"Where are you going?" he asked as he reached for his coat.

"Doctor's office," I said, hedging.

"Something wrong? You didn't say anything."

"I'm getting my tubes tied."

Tony froze with his jacket halfway on.

"Just make sure you're free," I said as breezily as I could manage. "I won't be in any condition to get home by myself."

Tony stared at me and then turned on his heel, slamming the door as he went. Little Tony cried in the next room.

When Tony came home from work, he hung up his coat, ate in silence, and went to bed early. He hardly spoke to me. But the luggage stayed in the closet, so I slept easier that night than I had in a long time. He might have been mad at me, but he didn't try to leave.

My friend Marcia went with me to the surgery. She was relieved I'd told Tony, although she was anxious that he hadn't come along. "He'll get over it," I assured her. In my head I added, *He'd better.*

I was given gas to knock me out, and my last thought was that I'd made the right decision when I agreed to have Little Tony. I hoped I was making the right choice now. The next thing I knew, I was in and out of consciousness. Marcia later told me that I kept asking for her, even though Tony had come to get me and had been sitting next to my bed all along. He sat, mute, as I mumbled incoherently. He was curt with the nurses who released me.

I was still light-headed during the car ride home. Tony drove in silence. He hardly looked at me until he parked the car and came around my side to get me. Tony practically carried me in the front door and deposited me in our wicker love seat. He arranged my pillows, tucked me in, and left me to fend for myself.

Several times a day as I recovered, he would pass through the living room, check to make sure I had water, clean up any dishes, and make sure I looked OK. The only words he said were "Are you drinking enough water?" or "Have you had anything to eat?" or "Can I get you something?" Beyond that, he didn't speak to me for days.

Of course I worried that he wouldn't come around. What I had told Marcia was still true: if Tony couldn't live with my choice, then I'd have to find a way to live without him.

A week after my surgery, Tony turned the lights out on his way to bed and then came back out to the living room. "Are you coming to bed?" he asked.

I looked up to where he stood silhouetted by the hall light. "You tell me," I said. I'd compromised with him when it came to Little Tony. It was his turn to yield.

"The bed's too big," Tony said at last.

I smiled into my pillow. Then I got up and carried my blankets back to our room. We lay on opposite sides of the bed, not touching, but that was all right. We'd called a truce. That was the first step on the road back to normalcy.

# CHAPTER EIGHT

In 1990, when Ellie was five and Little Tony was about six months old, Big Tony made a proposition over dinner. "Why don't we move to Washington?"

I paused with my fork halfway to my mouth and looked up at him. He seemed to be completely in earnest. I slowly lowered my fork back to the plate.

"Where's Washington?" Ellie cut in.

"Washington, DC," Tony said grandly. "The capital city."

"Why Washington, DC?" I asked, still stunned.

"We could make a new start, have an adventure, see a new side of life. It's a big city, but it's a different flavor than New York. I could find work there no problem."

"What about me?"

Tony leaned in. "You wouldn't have to work. You could stay home with the kids for a while until they get a little bigger. When Little Tony's big enough for day care, you could look for a job you really like." It was obvious to me that my husband had put a lot of thought into this, and from the broad grin on his face, it was just as apparent that he really wanted this opportunity.

I wasn't so sure. This plan didn't sit well with me for a dozen reasons. I liked the independence of having a job, especially one I was good at. I liked living close to my mother. I had friends in New York. I liked our apartment. I liked our life.

As I looked at my husband's smile and took in my daughter's sudden interest, I wondered if I was being selfish. After all, this was the most important part of my life. As long as I had my family with me, I told myself, I could learn to be happy anywhere. Right? And maybe we could find a neighborhood that would be a better place for Ellie and Little Tony to grow up than our street in Harlem. "I'll think about it," I said.

Tony grinned, and we both knew he would win this one.

When I told my parents we were moving, my father pursed his lips. My mother tried to be a little more supportive, but I could tell she didn't like the idea. "Who will take care of the kids?" she asked.

"I will," I said. Her support would be the thing I would miss most after we moved. I'd known that since Tony's suggestion that we relocate.

We already had a routine with the kids. I dropped them off with my parents on my way to work, and my mother spent the day taking care of them. I picked them up on my way home. By the time I got there, both kids were usually bathed and ready to leave. My mom loved having them over, and I was grateful for her help. I actually thought the kids were in better hands with her than with me. I couldn't imagine leaving the kids with someone I didn't trust. My history made me wary of other people's motives. My mom watched the kids because she loved them, but how would I ever find someone I'd be comfortable passing the kids off to for hours at a time in DC?

"Good luck," my mother said, kissing my cheeks. "I wish you the best, Carmen."

I wanted to stay with my mother, but I also wanted Tony to be happy. If he wanted to move to DC, then I'd make the move for him.

We didn't move right away. Tony wanted to visit first so that we could get a feel for the area and decide where we wanted to live. We started by visiting neighborhoods and staying in hotels near areas we thought we'd like.

We checked out barbershops Tony thought he might want to work in.

About a week into this adventure, Tony left us in the hotel room to go look at another local barbershop. "I won't be too long," he said. "Get some rest. We can go out later this afternoon to see more of the neighborhood."

I waved him off, expecting a quiet hour or two with the kids. I could get Little Tony down for a nap and maybe Ellie, too, if I was lucky. I was wrong.

About fifteen minutes after Tony left, I heard a knock at the door. I got up and answered it, not even bothering to look through the peephole. It was a maid whom I'd seen a few times over the last few days. "Would you like the room cleaned?" she asked.

I glanced over my shoulder at the rumpled, lived-in room. "Is it all right if we stay here while you do it?" I asked. Little Tony was almost settled, and I didn't want to wake him up just to get the room tidied.

The maid hesitated and then shrugged. "If you want. I don't mind."

Although the place was technically a hotel, each room opened onto an outdoor walkway. People could come and go to their rooms as they pleased without having to pass through a lobby. The maid left her cart in the covered walkway between rooms and came in to assess the chaos. "I'll need a few things from the cart," she said before stepping back out to the hallway. I was watching the kids and not paying much attention to what she was doing. She didn't need to answer to me. I was just grateful that someone else was willing to tidy up the room for me.

As far as anyone can prove, the maid did exactly what she said she would do. Maybe she only stepped out to pick up a bottle of glass cleaner and fresh towels. Maybe I only imagined the other possibilities: the whistle or gesture over the balcony to a car waiting below, the message hissed down the hallway: *She's alone.* All I know for sure is that the maid stepped back into our room and for a minute or two carried on with her work as I all but ignored her. Then the slightly ajar door was flung open so hard the windows rattled. The maid shrieked as two men shoved their way into the room. I caught a glimpse of their faces and had no idea who they were.

One man appeared to be holding a gun. The maid opened her mouth again, but no sound came out. Ellie shrieked, and both men turned toward her. Before I could move, the maid had covered Ellie's mouth and was dragging her into the bathroom. I heard soft whimpers through the door and the maid's voice faintly repeating, "Hush…it's OK. We'll be OK."

Little Tony was now crying from the sound of the door slamming open. I lurched toward the bed to grab him, but one of the men got there first.

"Shut him up," hissed his partner, the one with the gun. "We don't need anyone coming to investigate."

Everything happened so fast that I hardly understood what was going on, but when that man lifted a pillow from the bed, time seemed to stop. He pressed the pillow down on my son's face. I didn't think about what would happen to me. I didn't worry about the gun or wonder if the second man might be armed, too. Before I could consider any of this, I had leaped toward the man trying to smother Little Tony and clawed at his arms. "Not my baby!" I told him. "Not my baby!" I didn't scream the words. Some instinct must have told me that if I raised my voice, they'd try to shut me up, too.

Clearly startled by my ferocity, the man holding the pillow stepped back, and I grabbed Little Tony to my chest. He whined and wriggled in my arms. *Thank God. Thank God.* I turned toward the bathroom, but before I'd taken two steps, the other man had crossed the room toward me. He raised his fist—the one holding the gun. I froze.

Instead of aiming at me, he brought the butt of the gun down on my face once, twice, three times. I thought of Cory and of broken glass. When he raised the gun again, I darted toward the bathroom door, but the handle wouldn't turn. I was glad the maid had thought to lock my daughter in but was terrified that my son and I were now trapped on the other side with these men.

"Please," I pleaded. "Please..." The lock clicked open. I stumbled into the bathroom, slamming the door behind me and locking it again.

The men didn't come after us. We heard them on the other side of the door, tossing the room around and going through our stuff to see what might be of value to them. Tony had a lot of jewelry, and we had some cash. I looked down at my baby and at my daughter, who was crying silently next to the bathtub. *Let them take everything*, I thought. The most valuable things in the room were already with me.

I tasted blood and reached up to discover that my face was smeared with it. My hands shook. Maybe these guys would be content to take Tony's gold chains, but I'd seen their faces. I looked at the maid, who still hugged my daughter, and saw fear in her expression. I fished my pager out of my pocket. I needed my knight. I needed my husband.

By the time Tony arrived, the guys had gone. The rest of us were still huddled in the bathroom, shaking and crying, shocked by the seeming randomness of the attack. "Oh my God," my husband said, gaping at the wound on my face. "Oh my God, Carmen."

I was unable to put the horror into words, so I simply clutched my baby and didn't speak.

"I'll call an ambulance," Tony said.

While he made the call, I sneaked a glance at the woman who had saved my daughter. But had she really? She seemed anxious and wouldn't look me in the eye. I started to think about what had just occurred. She had shown up almost as soon as Tony had left, almost as if she'd been waiting for him to leave. Could she have been in on it somehow? Had she seen my husband's jewelry sitting in the room and chosen us as marks?

"The ambulance is on its way," Tony said.

I shook my head, trying to clear the thought away. I'd just been attacked. Maybe I was being paranoid. We waited for what seemed an awfully long time. The adrenaline wore off, and my head started to pound. I was still bleeding, and whenever I wiped a damp washcloth across my forehead, the white cloth came away bloody. The whole ordeal seemed unreal.

"This is taking too long," Tony said suddenly. "Get in the car. I'll take you to the ER."

"I'm not sure you should drive," I said, trying to stay reasonable, since nobody else seemed to be.

"Carmen," he said, his eyes sweeping my face. I must have looked pretty bad.

"All right," I said, "let's go." I didn't want to wait in that room for one more second anyway.

Tony's hands shook as he drove. A few streets from the hotel, he didn't hit the brakes in time and rear-ended somebody's car. It was barely a tap, but the guy got out in a huff and took a few steps toward us, clearly ready to start a fight with the idiot who'd dinged his car. Tony got out, too, hands held up. "I'm sorry, man," he said. His voice broke a little, and I thought he was about to really lose it. "My wife was just attacked, and we're on our way to the hospital. She needs stitches."

The other driver glanced through the windshield at me, and his face softened. "Hey, forget it. It's fine," he said. "Just be careful with her, all right?"

I clung to Little Tony, who was still crying. Ellie made soft whimpering noises in the backseat. When Tony got back into the driver's seat, he took a huge breath. I saw two things in his face: fear that someone really could have hurt us and that he wouldn't have been able to protect us, and anger that someone would dare come after his family. I understood exactly how he felt.

For all the blood, the cut on my head wasn't as bad as it looked. It left a little scar—the only visible scar that any of us suffered as a reminder of that day—although the incident affected us all deeply. It didn't change Tony's mind, though. He still wanted to move to Washington, and he was determined to find someplace where we would all feel safe.

I headed back to New York and crashed with my parents for a few weeks while Tony sorted everything out. My parents all but said *I told you so.* By the time Tony sent for us, I was happy to escape their silent judgment.

The attack wasn't Tony's fault or even a problem with DC in particular. An attack like that could have happened in New York just as easily. I headed to our new home, kids in tow and ready to put the whole thing behind me. It hadn't escaped me that the maid had apparently quit her job two days after the attack. I was sure she'd had something to do with it, and I vowed to be more careful in the future.

About a month later, Tony and I went to the mall to look for furnishings for the new apartment. "No lawn furniture," Tony joked, and I rolled my eyes. We wandered aimlessly between stores, trying to decide which couch we wanted. I glimpsed a familiar face, and my heart pounded. I turned away slowly, trying to look without making it obvious that I was looking. It was the man who'd tried to smother Little Tony. Standing right next to him was his companion, the one who'd clobbered me with the butt of the gun. "Carmen, what the hell?" Tony asked, and I realized I was shaking.

"Let's go," I said.

"Go where?" he asked.

"Let's just get out of here."

My husband shrugged and led me from the mall to our car. "What's wrong?" he asked. "What happened in there?"

I hugged myself. "I saw the guys." He raised his eyebrows. "The guys from the hotel," I explained.

Tony stood up very straight. His face changed, as if he were putting on a mask. He became someone I didn't know. Without a word, he opened the trunk and took out a baseball bat we kept in the car for emergencies. I watched, unable to move, as he went back into the mall. *Part of me hoped he'd find those guys.* After what they'd done to my family—and worse, what they'd tried to do—I felt they deserved whatever they got.

Another much more rational part of my brain was relieved when my husband came back, bat in hand, and admitted that he couldn't find them. He probably hadn't gotten a good enough look at them the first time, but I wasn't about to go back in and point them out. We got into the car and headed home, both shaken but for different reasons. It had occurred to me before that the guys were lucky Tony wasn't there when they barged in, but I hadn't realized I'd also been lucky that Tony wasn't there. Tony would have tried to fight them. At least one of them had a gun. They'd have killed us all.

Right from the beginning, Tony was my protector. That was his natural impulse. Seeing his anger, though, made me realize that sometimes his desire to protect us might be the very thing that got us hurt. My only thought had been to get the kids out of the way. Tony's only thought would have been to fend off the threat. For once, I was glad that bullies were so often cowards. The thieves obviously saw me as harmless, which saved my life.

It floored me to realize that my husband's tough, unwavering attitude very easily could have cost him his family.

# CHAPTER NINE

Tony and I lived in Washington for about a year. Tony wanted to experience a new city, and I played along, but the truth was that I'd never really wanted to move; after what had happened in the hotel, not much could have changed my mind. Juggling the kids was a full-time job that didn't pay. I was glad to spend time with them, but things had been much easier back home in New York. After a year, Tony saw that I was miserable and agreed to move back home.

I was thrilled to be back. We were near my family, I had my mother's support again, and I was able to go back to work. It was easy to get back into the swing of things. I'd missed having my independence. *This is how life should be*, I thought. Tony and I thrived, the kids were happy, and overall things seemed right with the world. I was content. I felt safer in New York. For once, my life was going smoothly. I wondered how long it would last.

I had a childhood friend who was very dear to my heart. She was one of my few really close friends. I was not very social because of my upbringing, but she was one of the rare people whom I felt I could trust completely. I'll call her Cindy. Her story isn't mine to tell, but some parts of her life completely changed mine in ways I never could have predicted.

Cindy was intelligent, hardworking, and motivated. Her only problem was her self-esteem. She didn't hold herself in high regard and tended to settle for men who, to my mind, weren't worth her time. Around the time Tony and I moved back to New York, she was dating a real loser. Let's call him Gil.

Gil lived in a homeless shelter, which wasn't the real problem. The problem was his laziness, bad attitude, and casual disregard for a woman who was far better than he deserved. Cindy just wanted someone to care about her, and Gil happened to have come along at the right time. She was willing to settle for anyone who sweet-talked her.

"You should drop him," I advised her. "He's no good."

"He's not as bad as you think," Cindy replied, "and he really cares about me."

I rolled my eyes.

Cindy sighed. "I see how you are with Tony. I want that, too."

"We fight about stupid things all the time!"

"But you love each other." Cindy looked at me intently. "And you're happy together."

I admitted that this was true.

"I just don't want to be lonely anymore," Cindy said.

I understood that and wanted Cindy to be happy. I let it go. After all, people had warned me off Tony, and look how that turned out. Maybe there was a side to Gil I didn't know. As it happened, there was, and it wouldn't be long before that side turned up.

Tony told me how it went down. It happened at the barbershop while I was at work, but I knew Tony, and I knew Gil, and I could fill in the blanks from what Tony told me afterward.

Tony always said that when someone sat down in his barbershop chair, he would become both a stylist and a psychologist. People would say things they wouldn't dream of saying to a near stranger under any other circumstances. "How's Cindy?" Tony asked Gil. He didn't know much else about Gil's life, and the fact that Gil was dating Cindy was one of the only things my husband liked about the man.

"Good for the moment," Gil said.

Tony was a little surprised by this remark. "Is that likely to change?"

"Well, I'm going to rob her," Gil said.

The scissors jumped a little in Tony's hand, but he went back to cutting. Gil might have been joking, even if my husband couldn't see the punch line. "She won't like that," Tony said.

"No," Gil said. "She'll probably go to the police, I guess. Maybe I should kill her so she doesn't make trouble for me afterward."

Tony had told me on our first date how he felt about men who bullied women. He clutched the scissors tighter in his hand. He wasn't cutting anymore. "That's not funny, man," he said, still trying to brush it off.

"I'm just thinking out loud here," Gil said. "She trusts me, you know? Robbing her is one thing. It wouldn't be hard, but she'd know it was me. Unless I went off the radar, she'd be able to find me. I wouldn't do well in prison, man. Seeing how things stand, I might have to kill her, or it'll be a real mess." He said it as if it was nothing, as if my friend was nobody. He also said it like he meant it.

Tony was almost positive Gil was serious as he looked at him in the barbershop mirror. Slowly, very slowly, he turned Gil's chair around so he could look at him eye to eye. Yes, Gil was serious. Tony was sure of it. "That's enough, Gil."

"OK, OK," Gil said, laughing it off. "See you later, man." He walked out the door, and it was all Tony could do to keep from grabbing him by the collar and hauling him back in.

Maybe Gil was just running his mouth. Tony didn't really believe it was all in jest, but he wanted to, so he didn't follow the man out. Tony tried to put the conversation out of his mind, but it nagged at him all day. By the time the shop was closing up, he'd managed to calm down a little. He could go home, have dinner, and decide whether or not to tell anyone about what Gil had said. As he was locking up, he heard a knock on the window and looked up to see Gil standing there and waving.

Tony went out the front door. "What's up?" he asked, trying to keep cool. He hoped Gil had come back to apologize for the tasteless joke.

"Hey, I want to show you something," Gil said. He waved my husband closer, opening his jacket to reveal the black butt of a handgun. "Just bought this piece. Pretty sweet, huh?"

"What do you need a gun for?" Tony asked. I can picture his face and how calm he must have seemed when inside he was burning with rage.

Gil stepped even closer and lowered his voice. "It's going down tonight," he said. "I think it's time. I feel ready."

Tony looked down again at the gun, only an arm's length away. "It's not funny, Gil. Cindy loves you. She'd be hurt if she knew you were talking like this."

"Not as hurt as she's going to be," Gil said with a grin..

Tony gritted his teeth. A more timid man might not have gotten involved. A less impulsive man might have told Cindy about the conversation before Gil had time to act. A wiser man might have called the police.

Tony did none of those things. He wasn't thinking about consequences. He was thinking that a very dear friend of mine was in danger and about what it would mean to me if anything were to happen to her. If Cindy were hurt, then I would be hurt. If she were killed, the grief would cut through me. I'd had enough grief. He wanted to spare me that.

He had no idea how much grief he would cause me that day.

I was home when the phone rang. I was surprised to hear Tony's voice on the other end of the line. He sounded shaky and out of breath. "What's wrong?" I asked. "Did something happen?"

"Ma," he said. That was what he always called me: Ma. There was a pause, and then a deep breath echoed in the receiver. "Ma," he repeated, "I got arrested."

"Arrested?" I closed my eyes and leaned against the kitchen counter, trying to process something that didn't make sense. "Arrested for what?"

"I shot Gil."

What could I say to that?

"With his own gun," he added.

"Why?" I paused. This wasn't a conversation I wanted to be having over the phone. This wasn't a conversation I wanted to have at all. I could ask about his reasons later, but only one question would tell me how bad things really were. "Is Gil…" I couldn't say it.

Tony could. "Dead? No." He spoke flatly, but my stomach unclenched just a little.

I needed time to organize my thoughts and pull myself together. "Tell me where you are." He gave me the address. "I'm on my way."

I had collected the kids from my mom's place on my way home from work, but now I packed them right up again. My mother was surprised to see me back at her apartment, but she took one look at me and must have understood that something big had happened. She herded the kids through the door without a word. My mother was my backbone, always.

There was no fighting the charges. There was nothing to fight. Tony was guilty. There were witnesses—end of story. We were lucky enough to be able to hire an attorney rather than being assigned a public defender. The attorney explained that we had two choices. One, we could take the case to trial. "I don't recommend you do this," she cautioned us. "It would be a big risk. Courts tend to be stacked against black men who are on trial for violent crimes, and in the end, you're likely to spend a longer time in prison."

Two, she said, Tony could take a plea bargain and settle out of court. "You're likely to get a shorter sentence," our lawyer advised us. "Since there's no question of your guilt, this is probably the better route to take." There was no question then of whether Tony would go to prison. It was just a matter of how long he'd be there.

Tony followed the lawyer's advice and took the plea bargain. He was very realistic about the whole process. I wished he'd been as rational and clearheaded before he shot Gil. I kept working throughout all this, and I kept my mouth shut. I didn't tell anyone what was happening to my family. It was nobody's business but ours.

*I didn't talk about it. Twelve years, they told me. For twelve years, my husband would be incarcerated and I would have to find a way to live without him.*

"I'm so sorry, Carmen," my mother said. We sat at her old kitchen table in the one room of the apartment that had always been her domain. I felt safe with her, as if she could undo everything that was happening and put the mess of my life back in order.

"I don't know what I'll do without him," I said miserably.

My mother pursed her lips and leaned over to rub my shoulders. "Have you thought about...your options?" she asked softly.

"I feel like I've thought of everything." I rubbed my forehead. "I'm basically a single mother. How will I stay afloat?"

"Maybe you should be a single mother."

I turned toward her. "I just said—"

She laid a hand on my arm, and I fell silent.

"Do you really want to be married to a criminal?" my mother asked.

I opened my mouth and quickly closed it again. I thought I'd considered every possibility, but this one was new to me. It hadn't occurred to me to divorce Tony.

"Twelve years is a long time to wait. And for what? Your kids will practically grow up without a father. You'll be raising them alone. You could be married to someone else long before he gets out."

"But I love Tony." It sounded like a weak argument against her logic.

"I know you do," my mother said, "but you have children to think about. Not to mention bills. You have your own life."

If my father had introduced the idea, I'd have laughed in his face, but my mother was another matter.

She loved me, and I knew she was looking out for me. "I'll think about it," I told her.

She patted my arm. "That's all I'm asking.

Once Tony was sentenced, I had to find a job imme-diately. Ellie and Little Tony needed stability, and I was the only person who could provide that. She was five years old, and he was one. I landed an inter-view at a radiology office in Manhattan. It was a hot August day, so I decided not to wear panty hose for the interview. I was sitting in the waiting area when I heard my name. As I approached a stunning lady, I said to myself, *You should have worn the panty hose.* She introduced herself to me as the practice manager. Her name was Pat. Her suit was Chanel, and her hair, nails, and makeup were flawless. I kept telling myself *You should have worn panty hose: there's no way you'll get this job.* After an hour, she thanked me for coming in and said someone would be calling me one way or another. I thanked her and went home. The train ride home was extremely depressing. I received a call from Pat the following day. The job was mine. This job would become my home for the next twenty-two years.

My mother's advice was still ringing in my ears when I went to see Tony in prison for the first time. I was already feeling the stress of parenting alone as well as the loneliness of keeping a secret from all my coworkers and most of my acquaintances.

It was almost a ten-hour bus ride to the correctional facility. I didn't have a car, so I had to catch a bus at five in the morning. I'd booked a hotel for that night, knowing I would have another ten-hour bus ride the next day to get back home. I didn't know what to expect at the correctional facility and I didn't know what to tell the kids, so I decided they would stay with my mother. All I said was that I was leaving to see their dad.

I transferred to another bus to get to the correctional facility. Several women formed a group at the front of the bus, most of them dressed as though they were going to a club. "I'm going to see my man!" one hooted. The others applauded.

I looked away. I could never feel that casual about my husband's situation—if he remained my husband, that is. I was still turning the word *divorce* over in my mind.

When we got to the correctional facility, the other women were let in one at a time. Each visitor stepped into an intermediary room; bars then closed behind each of us, and then bars on the other side opened to let us into the visiting room. When it was my turn to wait in the room, caught between bars, I hugged myself. I couldn't have gotten out if I'd wanted to.

I jumped when the doors closed behind me. An assortment of tables and mismatched plastic chairs filled the large visitors' room. The women waited at separate tables, sometimes calling out to one another. I saw other visitors whom I didn't recognize from the bus, and even a few families. I tried to picture my own children shut in with us there. The thought made me feel sick.

Every time a prisoner was buzzed in, I jumped, expecting to see Tony. What would I say? But the first two or three men to walk through the door wandered to other tables, where their wives or girlfriends or families greeted them. By the time Tony was buzzed through, my nerves were raw. Could I really do this for *years* to come?

Tony sat down across from me. His eyes looked sunken, and I could tell he hadn't been sleeping. "How is it?" I asked, flinching at how stupid the question must have sounded. I kept turning my eyes toward the cheap foam panels that formed the ceiling just so I wouldn't have to make much eye contact with him.

Tony smiled sadly. "Don't worry about me, Ma. Just take care of yourself."

"I'm trying," I said. There was silence.

Tony examined my face. I hated having to see him dressed in orange in a room he couldn't leave. I wanted to go back to the way we were, but that was one thing I couldn't change. The only person whose future I could control was my own. "I want you to know you can leave me," he said suddenly. The words tumbled from his mouth as if he'd geared up to say them and now had to get them all out at once before he changed his mind. "I won't blame you. Nobody will. If something happened to you while I was in here, I'd never forgive myself. Whatever you have to do to take care of yourself, to keep yourself happy, do it. Don't worry about me. I'll look out for me. Worry about you."

I sighed. "That's what my mother said."

He wilted a little bit. I guess he'd have preferred if I'd told him that the idea hadn't occurred to me and that I would be unquestioningly faithful forever no matter what. But that wasn't how I felt, so I didn't say it.

Silence settled between us, and I caught a few words from a neighboring table. The couple was deep in conversation, and sometimes one laughed at what the other said. I couldn't imagine being that at ease here. I felt certain I could never get used to this.

I imagined my other option—going on dates, looking for a man to help me raise my children, explaining that my ex was in prison. That was hard to imagine, too—me without Tony. But I'd be without Tony either way, no matter what I decided.

"Whatever you do," Tony said gruffly, "please don't keep the kids away. If my sister has to bring them, we'll make it work, but please…" His voice died, and I remembered the day we met, when he told me about his first daughter. I understood then how much Tracie mattered to him.

Sitting in the correctional facility that day, both of us surrounded by guards and bars, I knew how much Ellie and Little Tony meant to him, too. He wanted to be part of their lives, regardless of the circumstances. He was a good man, my husband. He always tried to do right by the people he loved, even if he sometimes went about it the wrong way. I sighed. "I love you, Tony. I wish you'd think with your head more, but you're here, and I..."

He rested his head in his hands, not looking at me.

"I'm going to try," I told him.

His eyes lifted to mine; other than that, he didn't move a muscle.

"I don't know if I can make this work, but I want it to, so I'm going to try."

Tony blinked at me. I didn't see tears in his eyes, but his relief was palpable.

"My mother's going to think I'm crazy," I told him.

"Maybe you are." He smiled, and a little of the hollowness left his face.

"It's starting to feel that way," I told him. I leaned back in my uncomfortable plastic chair furnished by the US prison system.

Tony's face was as soft as I'd ever seen it. "I'll always love you, Carmen," he said.

I was counting on that, because the idea of what life would be like when he was out again was going to have to sustain me for the next dozen years.

Did I wait because of guilt? Did I wait because of love? Did I love him too much? Tony was the father of my children. Was that why I stayed? I've thought about it for a long time, and the only answer I can come up with is that I waited because I truly loved this man. It was like Tony said in his letter to me when we first started dating: *It was in my heart for real.* It was a hard lesson, but we learned that the love between us was genuine. I knew I had a good man. I went against everything everyone advised me about at the time, and I hoped I was making the right decision. It would be a long wait, but I was always a fighter. I'd make it work.

# CHAPTER TEN

I t was one thing to say that *I* could make *it* work. It was another to actually live day to day with two kids on one salary. Waking up alone in bed was challenging. Managing the kids was exhausting.

I couldn't escape all the feelings that came along with being the only adult in the house, but the trickiest part by far was the money. I had to make one paycheck stretch as far as two had, and it simply couldn't be done. Some bills had to be paid every month, like power and rent, and I had to figure out which expenses I could cut back on to cover the rest.

The grocery bill was one place I had to make adjustments. I cut way back on how I shopped by tightening my belt both figuratively and literally. Before long, people seemed to notice. "Aren't you taking a lunch break today, Carmen?" my friend Ginger asked. We worked at the same radiology lab, and she was one of the few people I spent time with outside the office, so she tended to be more aware of my behavior than most of my coworkers were.

"No," I admitted, "not today."

"Still on a diet?" Ginger asked. "You look fantastic. You don't need to lose a single pound."

Pat, the manager who'd hired me and who knew more about me than anyone else at the office, glanced over at me with raised eyebrows.

"Maybe not, but I don't need to gain one, either," I said cheerily. "See you later!" I zipped away before either of them could ask any more questions.

The truth was that my refrigerator was practically empty. I had to pay the electric bill or phone bill or rent, or get something for the kids, or...

There was always some bill that needed to be paid. I could live without lunch. It wasn't as if we starved. The kids got lunch at school. They stayed with my mother after school and on the weekends. By the time I got home from work, dinner was always waiting for us. Mom fed the kids, and she fed me when I was around.

My empty fridge was just one thing my coworkers didn't know about me. Apart from Pat—who was too involved in my life to be kept in the dark—almost no one knew about what had happened with Tony. "He's away," I always said. "He's on a business trip," the kids would tell their friends. I didn't think of it as lying. It was our business.

My mother told me to be careful about what I said. "If you go around telling everyone and complaining about Tony and how hard things are, that's all people will think of when they look at him and when they look at you."

"That I'm the wife of a criminal?" I asked, feeling bitter.

"Things are more complicated than that, I know," my mother said soothingly, "but people are judgmental. When you walk out, walk with your head held high. You have nothing to be ashamed of. Nobody needs to know everything."

It was good advice, and I took it. Before long, I felt as if I were living two lives. There was professional Carmen, who did her work well and was always cheery in the office, and there was private Carmen, who raised two kids on one income and spent the weekends making long trips across the state to visit her husband in a correctional facility. Sometimes I felt like I was becoming two separate people. I went home to an empty bed, but nobody knew that.

We developed a weekend routine. I packed up the kids, booked a hotel, and took us all on a ten-hour bus ride to the Dannemora penitentiary far upstate, almost in Canada. I tried to make the outings as much like vacation as possible. I looked for hotels that had pools so the kids would have something to look forward to at night. I made sure the places we stayed had doors that opened onto a hallway, not the outdoors.

I couldn't imagine facing another attack like the one we'd survived in DC.

Sometimes Tony's daughter Tracie came with us. Her mother had no interest in traveling with her, but she allowed Tracie to come along on our trips. The kids and I never talked about why Tony was no longer home. They knew something was wrong, of course, and they knew that we kept to ourselves. I thought that if I didn't explain too much, then they wouldn't be as traumatized as I was when the doors shut us into the penitentiary.

"Are you excited to play games with Daddy?" I asked. Ellie nodded emphatically.

"I wanna swim in the pool," Little Tony said.

"After we see Daddy," I reminded him. I couldn't believe how young the kids were now. Tony was three, and Ellie was eight.

He swung his feet above the floor of the bus. "I know, but I like the pool."

Tracie was quiet, staring out the window. As the oldest, I think she had the best sense of what it meant for Tony to be behind bars. And who knew what her mother had put into her head.

The kids napped on the bus. After the first two or three weekend trips, the same landscape wasn't enough to hold their attention during the long road trip. I would have preferred to sleep, but I couldn't let my guard down on the bus, especially with my kids in tow.

When we finally reached Dannemora, I herded the kids off the bus. They knew to stay close, but they watched the other passengers with some interest. In the last few months, a few of the women had become familiar to me. They were friendly with one another, and some probably would have been friendly with me, too, if I'd let them. I was never one of them, though. I didn't know how to be. I didn't want to be. *This is not who I am*, I kept reminding myself. *This is not who we are.*

The kids eventually seemed to get used to the system. They no longer flinched when the doors shut us in, even if I still did. Instead of waiting at a table and looking up whenever a prisoner was buzzed in, they made a beeline for the stack of approved games. We'd played every one of those stupid games more times than I cared to count, but it was a way to keep things normal when we were inside. *Backgammon. Trouble. Checkers. Chess. Lord, spare me another day of board games.*

When Tony was buzzed in that day, his face was lit up by a smile. Little Tony ran to greet him. Ellie followed more gracefully. Tracie sat next to me and placed a pack of playing cards on the table. "Somebody already took all the good games," she explained.

Tony sat with us, and for six hours we tried to be a normal family. The kids talked endlessly about school and their grandmother and friends and everything they had done that week. Then it was my turn. "I started that new program," I said. "I'm tired of being a secretary. I'm training to be a tech."

"That sounds like a better job," Tony said with sincerity.

"It'll be more fulfilling," I said, hedging. It would also pay better. The money was important, but it wasn't the only thing: I wanted to better myself to better my family. I wanted more from life than to work as a secretary forever.

Tony gave me a warm smile that almost hid how worn out he was. "You're something else, Carmen." If the kids noticed that he never talked about himself, then they didn't say so.

As the other inmates waved good-bye to their families, we packed up our cards. Tony gave us each a lingering hug. "I'm going to swim in the pool right after we leave," our son announced.

Tony laughed. "That sounds fun! Sometimes I wonder if you look forward to playing in the pool more than seeing me."

Little Tony hesitated. "I like playing games with you."

My husband shook his head and was led from the room. I shepherded the kids back out to the bus, and that was it for the week. The hours we spent together were good, although I could happily spend the rest of my life without ever again looking at a deck of cards. It just wasn't enough to make up for twenty hours on the bus, weeks without lunch, or having to balance the checkbook to make sure I could cover the monthly bills.

While the kids clowned around in the pool that night, I watched from a chair. They were having a great time, but I knew they also felt the pressure building. *School, work, secrets, kids, prison, and nothing left over for myself. Something has to change, I told myself, or I'm really going to lose it.*

The change came in one of Tony's letters. He'd toed the line at the penitentiary, and as a result they were moving him closer to the city. The commute would be six hours—still long, but a lot shorter than the trip we'd been making. I was so relieved when I got the news that I cried in my mother's kitchen.

Around the same time, Tracie's mom informed me that her daughter would no longer be joining us. "I don't want that man in her life," she said, and that was that. Tony was heartbroken, but the heartbreak was balanced by a third surprise. As part of his new situation, he could apply to get a trailer for the weekend once every ninety days, as long as he remained a model inmate.

I saved up my vacation time until we knew the dates. Then I took the kids out of school and packed us up for four days in the trailer. The visits became markers for the seasons: spring visit, summer visit, fall visit, and then winter. Getting to the trailer was similar to getting into the visiting room. We had to go through the same level of security, but there were three big differences once we'd cleared the checkpoints. First, once we were inside the trailer, it was actually possible to forget for a while that we were on prison property. We could cook, relax, go to sleep, and wake up together. It was the closest we could get to feeling at home.

Second, we had privacy. I could feel the kids relax, and I soon realized that although we'd never talked about what it meant for their father to be in prison, they'd always been on edge before. In the winter they now got to play in the snow with their father, just like a normal family would on a normal snowy day.

Third—and this probably saved our marriage—Tony and I got to share the same bed for a few nights. I was glad to be able to meet him as a woman again. We had only a handful of nights together every year, but without them, our mere love for each other probably wouldn't have kept us together for much longer.

In a strange way, I think the tough times between visits brought us closer as a family. If our family's dynamic had gone on the way it had, we might have outgrown one another eventually. Those years were difficult, but they allowed us to test the reality of our relationship. We had to evaluate what was really important to us.

I reminded myself that everything happens for a reason and soon fell asleep beside my husband in the prison-approved trailer. *Even this.*

Every year my employer held a Christmas party, and every year I made up an excuse about why Tony couldn't make it. Finally, several years into Tony's sentence, my co-worker Ginger cornered me about it. I'd had a few glasses of eggnog, and she put another one in my hand. "So," she said, "I see Tony's not here again."

I sipped my eggnog and shook my head.

"Is he a figment of your imagination? I'm thinking he must be." She looked at me from the corner of her eye, smiling warmly as she said it. She was joking, of course, but I could tell she was fishing for some real information. I didn't think Ginger was being nosy. She always kept an eye on me at work, and I got the impression that she was asking about me because she cared, not because she was bored and wanted to poke around in my business.

Maybe it was the alcohol, or maybe it was intuition, but I took a chance. "Tony's in prison."

Her eyebrows shot up. "What? Who else knows?"

"Only Pat."

"So it's a secret." She sipped her own drink. "What's the deal?"

I explained the situation: not only why Tony was in prison, but also how we'd met, how I felt about him, and how hard we'd been working on our marriage while he was behind bars. I found the whole story spilling out of me; I cut myself off when other coworkers drifted by.

"Wow," Ginger said. "It's been years, and I never..." She paused. "Is Tony really worth all that?"

"He is," I said without hesitation.

"Then I trust your judgment," she said. "I trust you, and if you think he's worth it, then I believe you. Let me know if there's anything I can do to help, OK?"

Now I struggled for words. I just stared at her. I'd kept my personal life secret for years. It meant more than I could express to learn that someone whom I respected as much as Ginger would have such faith in me.

I didn't tell another soul at work or anywhere else about Tony for many years. Now that Pat and Ginger both knew the truth, however, they teamed up to check in on me and make sure I was OK. I felt comfortable having them both over to see my kids now, since I no longer had to worry that I would accidentally let something slip. Both being very Catholic ladies, they sent books, cards, and Bible verses to Tony.

For the first time since Tony had been arrested, I felt like my life belonged to me. I was no longer alone. I had friends I could trust. I still had to work just as hard to make ends meet, and I had to fight just as hard to keep my marriage together, but the weight of it all was no longer crushing me. I had a support network that extended beyond my family, and although this was hard-earned support, I was blessed with the friendships of these women. They would mean more to me in the coming years than I ever would have predicted.

# CHAPTER ELEVEN

Ellie and I were on our way to visit Tony. Little Tony was staying with a friend, but my daughter and I were making the long trip to see her father. We took the bus as we always did.

I was used to the other women who usually shared the bus, but on this particular visit a woman I did not recognize sat only a few seats away. She was reading a magazine, and I did a double take when I realized that it was porn. I turned, trying to situate myself between the woman and Ellie. Partway through the bus ride, the passenger started fondling herself. I ignored it as best I could, but by the time she was making enthusiastic sound effects, I'd had enough. "Excuse me," I said, as politely as I could, "but could you please put that away? My daughter's with me."

The woman rounded on me. "Who the f—k are you? You don't tell me what to do. You're not the boss."

"Hey!" called the driver. "None of that."

"Tell it to her!" the woman hollered. "I'm minding my own business, unlike *some* people!"

I narrowed my eyes at her and leaned closer. "I'm not playing. My kid doesn't need this, and I don't, either. If you don't like it, let's have a little chat when we get off the bus."

The moment the bus stopped, the woman scampered away from me. I figured she was all talk; I was a little relieved that I didn't have to deal with her. Still, my blood pressure was through the roof. Tony always hated public transit because, as he said, buses and subways were full of crazy people. I was feeling a little crazy myself. I took Ellie's hand and led her toward the entrance to the penitentiary. It was clear that I'd have to find a way to visit Tony that wouldn't involve taking the bus.

My brother Richie came to my apartment one day. He looked awfully pleased with himself as he strutted his way through the door and pulled faces at the kids, who were thrilled to see their favorite uncle. I was happy, too. Richie was the one sibling I could always count on and the one I could let my guard down around. "How are you doing, Carmen?" he asked.

"About the same." I didn't see any point in complaining.

Richie nodded knowingly. "If only there was something in your life to make things a little easier," he mused. "Something that would save you time and money."

I squinted at him. "Sounds like you're trying to sell me insurance."

"Me?" Richie scrunched his face up in a wounded expression. "How could you say that when I just bought you such a lovely present?"

Ellie said, "Present?" That was the magic word. "What is it?"

Richie reached into his pocket and jingled something. He grinned at me, waiting for a response, but I just crossed my arms and waited. At last he fished something from his pocket, held out his hand, and showed me what he'd brought. It was a car key. "It's a little bit old," he admitted, "and it's got some problems, but if you can find someone to take a look at it, you'll save a lot of time and bus fare."

"You bought me a car?" I asked.

"An old car," he repeated, "but beggars can't be choosers, right?" He winked at the kids.

Ellie looked at me with wide eyes; she was old enough now to appreciate the difference a car would make for us. But I hesitated. "I'm not sure I—"

"Oh, come on," said Richie, cutting me off. "I've only got one favorite sister. Just take it."

I held out my hand for the key. "Thanks, Richie," was all I could say. I didn't just mean *thanks* for the car. I meant *thanks* for everything.

"A little old" was an understatement. It was a white, beat-up Honda with more rust than paint. That car had all kinds of problems, but it ran. It just needed a lot of help to keep running. That was where my middle brother Frank came in.

I had never been to close with Frank. He was nine years older than me, and my parents pressured him into enlisting when he was a teenager. After that we always said that he became the United States of America's problem. He spent ten years in the service; by the time he came back, he was hooked on drugs and had a host of other problems. Frank's saving grace was his handiness. He'd gone to automotive school, so he offered to take care of the car for me. "Don't worry about it," he told me, obviously pleased to be able to offer help for once. "What's family for?"

Before long, I was relying on that car for everything. It was a huge relief not to have to take the bus to the prison anymore. I felt a lot more independent, and although I relied on my brothers for car maintenance and repairs, leaning on family felt a lot better than stumbling along on my own. I'd done my best to be there for my siblings, and it meant a lot that they were willing to be there for me. Family is in the heart. My family members were the first to teach me about the world. Oh, ain't that the truth?

The trouble started on our way back from visiting Tony one weekend. Something in the undercarriage was rattling and wouldn't stop. "Mom," complained Little Tony, "the car's doing that thing again."

"I'll take the car to Uncle Frank when we get home," I assured him. I wasn't too worried about the noise. The car made weird sounds all the time, and they usually didn't amount to much.

I took the car by my brother's place after work the next day. Frank started the car up and listened for the noise. "Oh, that doesn't sound too bad," he said. "I should have it back to you in a couple days."

I groaned inwardly at the thought of getting by without the car for a few days, but at least I would have it back by the weekend for our next trip to see my husband. Transportation within the city wasn't too bad. "Thanks," I said. "I appreciate it."

My brother saluted and then gave me a goofy grin. "You're welcome, sis."

I took the train home that night. The kids weren't thrilled that we'd be without the car for a while.

"I don't like the subway," complained Little Tony, sounding more like his dad than he knew.

"You should be grateful we even have a car," I reminded them. "Remember how it was before Uncle Richie gave it to us?" Ellie nodded solemnly. "Anyway, it's just a few days," I told them. "Frank will call me back by Tuesday, maybe Wednesday. Then we'll be back in business."

Tuesday came and went. When I didn't hear from my brother by Wednesday night, I gave him a call. The phone rang through to voice mail, and I left a message asking him to call me back. I knew my brother wasn't always on top of things, and his drug problem meant that he was sometimes hard to reach. Nevertheless, I knew he'd come through for me in his own time.

I heard nothing on Thursday, either. After calling Frank again, I tried Richie. "Have you heard anything?" I asked him. "I could go to his place, but—"

"I'll swing by and see what's up. He probably just fell behind and doesn't want to admit it isn't done yet." That sounded like Frank. I thanked Richie and went on with my day.

The phone rang a little while later, and I breathed a sigh of relief. I expected it to be Frank, finally calling about my car. "Hey," I said into the receiver.

Richie's voice answered, a definite note of anxiety in it. "Carmen, I'm calling from Frank's place."

My heart pounded. *Oh, God,* I thought. *He's over-dosed, he's been arrested, something's happened to him.*

"He isn't here," Richie said. "Some of his stuff's gone, too."

"A robbery?" I asked.

"No," Richie said, the hesitation clear in his voice. "It hasn't been tossed. It just looks like he left. And, uh, Carmen—the car isn't here."

"*My* car?"

"Yeah," Richie said. "Frank probably took it with him, wherever he went."

I slammed my fist down on the table. "Or he sold it!"

"Maybe," he said. Frank was always short of money. Richie said, "We'll find him. I promise. Don't worry."

Frank wasn't just the handy brother who was good with cars. He was also handy at making things disappear.

We started by calling hospitals. I was relieved after we didn't find Frank in an ER somewhere, but that meant we still had no idea where he'd gone.

"Maybe he's been arrested," I suggested, thinking of my vanished car. We called around, but the police had nothing for us.

Richie and I began a private investigation in search of our brother. We called his usual hangouts. We looked up his friends. We tried everyone we could think of, hoping something would turn up.

I dedicated my weekends to visiting Tony. Now my weeknights became dedicated to finding Frank. Between work, the kids, and the men in my family, I found myself again at the end of my rope. I was also back to using public transportation again. I alternated between being angry at my brother for putting me through all this and fearing that something horrible had happened and that we'd never see him again.

Three months after my brother disappeared, I came home to a blinking light on my answering machine. It was from Frank. As soon as I heard his voice, I screeched, "He's alive!" I then thought, *I'm gonna kill him.*

"Hey, Carmen," the message said, "I left your car nearby. The key's under the mat. You can take it back." He left an address in the Bronx, and that was it—no apology or explanation.

I called Richie at work. "Frank called," I said. "He left the car somewhere in the Bronx. I'm on my way to get it now."

Richie swore. "If someone else doesn't get it first. What is he thinking?" There was a moment of silence on the line as we both considered how many times we'd asked that very question in the last three months.

Miraculously, the car was still there when I showed up, the key under the mat just as Frank had promised. I collapsed into the front seat and rested my head on the steering wheel. "I can't believe I trusted you, Frank," I muttered to myself. He'd never have pulled that kind of crap while Tony was around, so why did he feel OK doing it to just me?

From then on, I decided, I wouldn't assume that other people's problems had anything to do with me. People might stab me in the back, but that didn't mean

I had to change who I was. For everyone who hurt me, someone else was kind to me. I could be angry for how my middle brother treated me or grateful for a brother who never left my side.

I sat up and let my head flop against the seat's headrest. "OK," I said aloud, "from this day on, I have only one brother."

I stuck the key in the ignition and started the car. The engine turned over without a hitch. The rattling noise in the undercarriage was gone. *OK, I have one and a half brothers.* But if I hadn't figured it out before, I knew now that I couldn't trust someone just because we shared the same blood.

# CHAPTER TWELVE

Marcia had been my friend since we were both twelve years old. Sometimes it seemed as if her family were just an extension of mine. When Marcia's sister finished sixth grade, my mother made her a graduation outfit. When Marcia had her little boy, my mother became his babysitter. Her son was only a year older than Ellie, so even once Mom started to look after my kids, Marcia's son still came over regularly. I was happy my childhood best friend was still such a big part of my life, almost as if she were the sister I'd wished for when I was little.

In the spring of 1995, Marcia announced that she was getting married. My mother and I were thrilled for her. Even though the wedding wouldn't be until late in the summer, Mom and I rushed out to buy our dresses right away. I was a bridesmaid, and I had everything lined up for the wedding months in advance. We wanted everything to be perfect for Marcia.

One day in April, I went to my parents' apartment after work to have dinner and pick up the kids. My mother, who always suffered terrible allergies, had developed some serious hives earlier that spring. As I watched her cook, something struck me as being a little odd. I leaned over in my chair to examine her more closely. Her skin looked almost shiny. I got up from the chair and moved a few steps closer. Something smelled out of place with the meal she was making. "Ma," I asked hesitantly, "is there a reason you smell like fried chicken?"

"Oh." She turned to me. Her eyes were partially swollen shut from the hives, and a smudge of something greasy was on her glasses. "It's just the Crisco oil."

"Crisco oil?"

She nodded. "Yes. For the hives."

I shook my head, mystified, and she gestured toward her kitchen cabinets. I opened the doors to discover several shelves devoted to cases and cases of Crisco oil. She was buying the stuff as if she had stock in the company. "Ma," I began.

"The doctor says it will take care of the hives. Just smear it on, bathe in it a few times, and this will clear right up. That's what he told me."

My mother, like everyone else in the neighborhood, had gone to the same local doctor for ages. He probably used the same equipment he'd bought when he first set up practice. She had a tendency not to question the voice of authority, so if the doctor told her to do something, she did it—even if he told her to bathe in Crisco oil. I rubbed my forehead. "And how long have you been doing this?"

She tapped her swollen face with one finger, thinking. "Two weeks."

"Has anything changed?"

"It takes time," she said defensively.

I eyed her up and down. "You've lost weight," I said.

"Only a little."

"Ma, you have great health insurance. Can we please go to a real doctor, a *good* doctor? I'll take you myself."

My mother crossed her arms and scowled.

"Ma, I work in medicine. Trust me."

She sighed. "Of course I trust you, Carmen. All right, we'll go see one of your fancy doctors."

"And no more Crisco oil."

"No more oil, at least until we know what your doctors say."

My mother's mistrust of doctors could be traced back to her failed surgery before Richie and I were born. I knew she'd only agreed to see one of the doctors I recommended because I would be her voice. That was a victory for me, but it was only the first step. I wanted my mother to see the best doctor possible, and I knew of one who had an excellent reputation.

His name was Dr. Miller, and I was determined that he would be my mother's new physician. Unfortunately for me, he was also one of the most popular doctors in the area. The waiting list to see him was months long, and my mother was suffering from terrible hives and continued weight loss.

I mentioned my troubles to my boss Pat, who nodded sympathetically. The next day at work, she tapped me on the shoulder. "I got your mother that appointment with Dr. Miller," she said.

I gaped at her. "How?"

"I told my mother," she said. "She had an appointment for a routine checkup with Dr. Miller in a few days. She made a later appointment and gave her old one to your mother, since she needs it more than my mother does."

"She didn't have to do that." I was shocked by this generosity.

"Of course she did, honey," said Pat. "She's Catholic."

My mother didn't appreciate the gesture as much as I did. Or, if she did, it was the outcome she didn't like. My mother, who was so loving with me and so content to let her husband rule the household, was a holy terror in the hospital. She stood less than five feet tall, but she knew how to pitch a fit when she thought a situation called for it.

X-rays and skin tests revealed that she was PPD-positive, which meant, among other things, that she had an increased potential to contract tuberculosis. "It's fairly common in some segments of the population," Dr. Miller assured me. "I'd like to keep her here for a few days and run some other tests, just to make sure it's nothing to be concerned about, but I think we can get these symptoms under control." It was my mother, not the symptoms, he should have been worried about.

The first day I left her to go to work, Richie called from the hospital. "You'd better get over here, Carmen, or I'm going to kill her."

By the time I arrived, Mom was making the sign of the cross over and over, hollering at some poor nurse in furious Spanish. "How much urine are you going to take?" she demanded.

I sighed and turned to the nurse. "What's going on?" I asked in English.

"I'm trying to take a blood sample," said the nurse, backing away from my mother's flailing arms.

My mother frowned at her. "Why does she want to do that? She doesn't need my blood, either. She just took some three hours ago. It hasn't changed in three hours!"

"She needs another sample, Ma," I said patiently. "They're monitoring you in case something *has* changed. That's the whole point."

My mother narrowed her eyes at me and then reluctantly extended her arm, permitting the nurse to take another blood sample.

"That's exactly what I told you!" exclaimed Richie. "How come we had to go through all this?"

"The difference," said my mother with dignity, "is that Carmen knows what she's talking about."

Dr. Miller cleared my mother for release a few days later with a clean bill of health. He gave her antihistamines for the hives; unlike with the Crisco prescription, she noticed an improvement right away.

With her health on the mend, we went right back to planning for Marcia's wedding. Now that I didn't have to worry about my mother, I also went back to being frustrated with my marriage. Tony hadn't done anything in particular. Nothing had changed. That was kind of the problem, really.

During the week, I thought about the wedding, school, and planning for the future. On the weekends I visited my husband, who was still years away from being released from prison. We'd played every approved board game a hundred times over, and I'd put thousands of miles on the car...and for what? I knew it was harder on Tony, of course, but that didn't make it any easier for me. After all, I wasn't the one who'd shot Gil without thinking of the consequences.

My family planned a big Fourth of July celebration that year, and all my siblings were home to join the festivities. My sister even came from Seattle with her daughters. It was the first time all five of us had been home since we were kids. None of this improved my mood. Having the whole family together only reminded me of how long it would be before my own little family would be reunited—and not just in a prison trailer.

My sister, as she always did, set me on edge. I avoided my oldest brother, since I was unable to forget what he'd done to me when I was six. My middle brother also wasn't in my best graces after the incident with the car.

I arrived late to the party. I'd just come from seeing Tony, and I arrived fuming. The visit had gone badly, and we'd exchanged hard words. It had been five years since this nightmare had started. We were both tired of the situation, and I had reached the end of my patience. I wasn't in a festive mood now. I would have preferred to just crawl under the covers, but I had promised my mother I would come. I waved my greetings to everyone and did my best to avoid conversation. My mother finally singled me out. "Is something wrong?"

"I'm so sick of this shit," I growled. "I hate it, and I quit. I hate the security and the jumpsuits, and I hate Boggle, and I hate the phone calls. I hate him never being here, and I'm done."

Mom nodded thoughtfully. "If you're sure, then you should tell Tony."

I wasn't sure, when she put it that way. Mom always had a way of using my own words back on me, rephrasing exactly what I was saying in a way that made me reconsider my choices. Her tone was always so calming and cool that it made whatever I'd said in the heat of the moment more real to me. As I watched my family, I couldn't help resenting them for being able to let loose and enjoy the holiday. I just wanted something to be easy for once.

Since the rest of my family was having such a great time together, they decided they should all go to the Six Flags Great Adventure amusement park in New Jersey. Ellie and Little Tony were thrilled, and my mother said she'd be happy to take them. They went during the week; I couldn't go, since my boss was on vacation. I was fine with that. I was still in a funk over the situation with Tony and in no mood to play nice with my siblings. If my kids and my mother could enjoy themselves, that would be great.

Mom called me that evening from the park. "Having a good time?" I asked.

My mother, who had been so happy to have her kids around her, laughed bitterly. "They paired me up with some older lady. I feel like I'm her babysitter, except she isn't any fun. I'd have fun with the kids, but—"

"Is something wrong, Ma?" I asked, cutting her off.

She sighed. "Nothing. Forget it. We'll see you tomorrow."

"I hope you have some fun," I said.

"Well, I'll try."

When they got home the next evening, my mother's mood hadn't improved. I walked into her kitchen and saw my sister-in-law Annette. She was my oldest brother's wife, and it didn't shock me when she looked guilty and snapped her mouth shut. She was always begging my mom for money. "Did you kids have a good time?" I asked.

"It was great!" cried Little Tony, hugging my knees.

"We had so much fun. Can we spend one more night?" begged Ellie. She would have stayed with my mother all the time if she had her way. "Please?"

My mother shook her head. "I'm too tired," she said, and she looked it.

"But—" Ellie began.

"Another day," I said gently. "Let's go." I stepped up to my mother and kissed her on the cheek. "I love you, Ma."

My sister-in-law waved but didn't speak. I bundled my kids into the car, and we drove home. All the while they chattered about the rides, things their cousins had said, what they ate, what they saw. My mood lifted a little. Regardless of my problems, I had great kids.

When we walked into our apartment, I found the answering machine's light blinking. *Probably Tony*, I thought with a grimace. It could wait, but I went over and pushed the button anyway, wondering what my husband would have to say that would be able to fix how I felt.

The message wasn't from Tony. It was my sister's voice that echoed from the speaker. "Carmen, you need to come now. We just called an ambulance. I think Mom's had a heart attack."

My kids had barely put down their overnight bags, and I snatched them up again. We headed down the apartment stairs at a run. *Not my mother,* I prayed. I'd done without a lot in the past few years, but my mother was my rock and cushion all at once. I needed her. I would always need her.

# CHAPTER THIRTEEN

I dropped my kids off with Tony's sister on my way to my parents' apartment. "It's my mother," I explained, and she didn't ask anything else. I got to the apartment at the same time as the ambulance and raced into my mother's room.

"She's stable," an EMT told me.

I released a breath I didn't know I was holding. "She sees Dr. Miller," I explained. "Is there any chance you can take her downtown to Saint Vincent's?"

The EMTs agreed, and I followed them down the stairs. The whole family was there, but nobody questioned that I would be the one riding in the ambulance.

A nurse at Saint Vincent's Catholic Medical Center later explained things more clearly. "She had a mild heart attack," she said. "Now she's stable and coherent and seems to have come out of it pretty well. Our main concern is that she might have a second heart attack.

That's not uncommon, and given how well she's doing now, I recommend a shot of Coumadin to thin her blood. That's routine procedure. It has something like a one-in-fifty-thousand risk of harmful side effects. Is she under a lot of stress right now?"

"My whole family's in town for a few days," I said.

She laughed. "That would do it!"

I explained the situation to my mother, who nodded. "I feel OK," she said, "but if they think it will stop this from happening again, then I'll take the shot."

My family arrived, and we talked it over with them as well. My dad looked lost and confused, and my siblings shrugged. "If it's safe, she should do it, right?" my sister said.

"There's practically no risk," I assured her. "Another heart attack might be worse than the last one. It's a preventive measure."

My family agreed, and they watched me sign the paperwork authorizing the shot. Mom was doing well, and once everyone was sure the heart attack hadn't done any lasting damage, they decided to go home. "There's nothing you can do here," my oldest brother said to me.

I flinched and turned away. "I'm not leaving my mother. Someone should stay. I know her doctor, and Mom's calmer when I'm here." The family agreed that I should stay, and they left. My mother was supposed to be moved to another room, so I waited with her. A few minutes before they transported her, I noticed something trickling from her nose. I dabbed a tissue against her face, and it came away red.

I paged the nurse, who examined her. "It's not unusual to see a little bleeding after a Coumadin shot." She sounded completely casual. "Blood thinners sometimes do this. I realize it's alarming, but I see this all the time." Evidently noticing my discomfort, she gave me a warm smile. "We'll keep an extra eye on her just in case."

Dr. Miller himself had my mother moved into her new room rather than letting the staff handle her transport on their own. My mother was in good hands, which put me at ease.

Hours passed, and my mother did not have a second heart attack. I calmed down, and gradually I became aware of how long I'd been wearing the same clothes and how disgusting I felt. I was still dressed for work, and I desperately needed a shower.

"Hey, Ma," I said, "I'm going to leave for a little bit, but I'll be back, OK?"

"Where are you going?" she asked. She sounded tired but otherwise sounded like her usual self.

"I need a shower. I'll just go back to your place."

"That's fine."

"Ma?" I chewed my lip. "You know that green suit of yours?"

"The one you always ask to borrow?"

"The one you never let me borrow."

"I know the suit. Yes, you can borrow it."

I grinned. "Do you need me to grab anything for you?"

She shook her head but then reconsidered. "Socks. My feet are cold."

I kissed her forehead. "I love you, Ma."

"I love you, too, Carmen," she murmured. Those were the last words my mother ever said to me.

By the time I got back to the hospital at 8:30 a.m., my mother's brain was bleeding. She was in a coma. It wasn't the heart attack that did it. It was the subdural: the Coumadin shot I'd authorized. *Almost without risk*, I kept telling myself. *A one-in-fifty-thousand chance of disaster.*

One in fifty thousand, and my mother was the one. I didn't leave the hospital for the next week. My boss Pat was still on vacation, but I called the office and told them what had happened. If I lost my job, so be it. That idea didn't scare me nearly as much as the thought that I'd lost my mother. I spent all my time in the waiting room or the chapel, praying for a miracle. My siblings came in shifts, mostly to make sure I ate something.

One night, when my sister was with me, I saw the medical director leave the elevator. I nudged my sister awake as he made a beeline for us. "Are you living here?" he asked.

"More or less," I admitted.

"I'll have someone set up a cot for you in my office," he said. "We're all praying with you."

Word had spread about my mother's condition, and aunts, uncles, and cousins were coming from all over. At first people came to express their condolences, but before long, they were chatting with folks they hadn't seen in years, joking about old times and family lore. "Get out," I said at last. "This isn't a joke. This isn't a reunion. Do this on your own time."

People left and didn't come back, and that was fine with me. Some of my cousins threatened to never talk to me again, and that was fine as well. I wasn't worried about anyone but my mother. I didn't have room in my head or my heart for anything else.

I needed to hear from Tony. We hadn't spoken since my blowup on the Fourth of July, and I needed someone to support me. I was able to get word to the prison chaplain to explain the situation, and a friend of ours was permitted to conference-call Tony so that I could speak to him from the hospital phone. I broke down when I heard his voice, bawling as I leaned against the pay phone.

I put our fight behind me. It was nothing. I needed him more than I ever had before.

As we sat in the hospital waiting room the next day, the elevator door opened. I was vaguely aware of a woman in flip-flops stepping out. My eyes wandered aimlessly up to her face, and I did a double take. It was my boss

Pat, still dressed for the beach. Ginger was right behind her. "Oh, Carmen," Pat said, and she hugged me. She was always the softer of the two.

Ginger was the tough one. "I'm going to find out what's going on. Wait here." I'd been doing nothing but waiting.

Pat explained, "The hospital director called. He said you'd been sleeping in his office and that you might need us. Well, here we are, honey. I'm so sorry."

I felt totally alone from the last week. I said, "It means a lot, you coming here. Thank you." I groped for more words, but there were none.

Ginger reappeared, looking thin-lipped and grim.

"What did they say?" Pat asked.

Ginger held her arms out to me, and I got up to hug her. "Oh, Carmen," she said. "I don't know how to say this. Your mother—"

I held tight to her, waiting for her news to come down.

"She's brain-dead…completely. No function at all."

Pat and Ginger had propped me up before, but that was the first time I'd ever needed them to physically hold me up. I went limp in their arms.

My mother always said, "You'll be the first to know when I leave." I never took those words very seriously. I thought she meant she'd tell me first if she planned to divorce my father. She was right, though. I was the first to know she was gone, and it was my job to tell everyone else in the family. "So now what?" my middle brother asked.

"Now we have to decide what to do," I said. "Her body is still functioning. They can keep it alive with machines."

"*It*," said my father, looking as lost as I felt.

"It's not really her," I said. "She isn't in there." I'd felt it, standing beside her bed. Her heart was beating, but she was no longer there. She had gone somewhere else.

Richie took my hand. "What should we do?"

I remembered the Crisco oil and the blood taken at the hospital a few months ago. My mother had believed in me then. She always listened when I talked, and she'd listened when I'd told her about the Coumadin shot. It was the shot that had killed her, and I was the one who'd convinced her she needed it. I sighed. "I think we should unplug her. This isn't what she'd want. It feels selfish to wait for a miracle while she's..." I trailed off, but the rest of my family nodded in understanding.

I was surprised that nobody made a stink. For once, we were all on the same page. "Some of the aunts and uncles won't like it," my oldest brother pointed out. "You know—religious grounds. But I think you're right."

I looked away from him, almost resentful of his support. "Thank you."

If we had thought there was any chance of her coming back to us, we would have fought, even if she wasn't completely her old self. These days you hear about the odd miracle of someone who's on a machine for five or ten years who suddenly wakes up one day feeling perfectly fine. I'll always wonder if my mother had a chance, but when I looked at her in that hospital bed, I saw reality. *What kind of quality of life would she have? What would her chances be?*

I signed the paperwork authorizing the nurses to pull the plug on the life-support machines. My whole family agreed, but I had become our voice. Some of our cousins and aunts who disagreed—who saw our choice as a lack of faith—blamed me for what my siblings and I decided as a unit. It felt like the right decision, even though I would have done anything to keep her in my life.

I was twenty-seven years old. My mother was fifty-six. We were both too young. I signed the papers. We let my mother's body die.

My friend Marcia's little boy cried when she told him about my mother's passing. It was as though he'd lost a grandmother. It was harder with my own children. Little Tony understood that something was wrong, mostly because people kept crying, but he was only four. In a few years, he'd barely remember his grandmother.

Ellie was nine, and she understood better. "Why?" she asked me, crying when I told her that her grand-mother was gone. I had no answer.

I told Marcia I couldn't be in her wedding, which was only two weeks later. Another person might have been upset or hurt, but Marcia understood what my mother meant to me and never once made me feel bad about withdrawing. I went as a guest, but I couldn't put on an act for anyone. I was worn out, empty. I had nothing left. All the happiness and hope my mother and I had felt a few weeks earlier when we talked about the wedding now felt like a dream. Or else this felt like a dream. One of them couldn't be real.

Suddenly I longed for the days when an incarcer-ated husband was the heaviest of my burdens.

I couldn't stop replaying memories of my mother in my head. I wanted to remember all the times when we'd been happy together instead of just feeling lonely with-out her. One event in particular kept coming to mind.

When I was a little girl, a family friend gave me some money at Christmas. Richie got some, too. I don't think the others did, maybe because they were so much older, but I don't remember for sure. I had my heart set on a doll, an off-brand Barbie. I'd asked for one for Christmas, but my parents didn't have the money to justify such an expensive gift—not even the off-brand variety. Now, though, I could buy my own. I knew just the one I wanted.

I looked at Richie, who was holding his own money, and we grinned like fools. What wealth we had! What possibility! Then I looked at my mother. There were no presents for her, and although it was a little thing, almost a silly thing, I saw pain in her face. I saw sadness.

She was always doing things for us. I looked at my money, and then I looked at Richie. We pooled our few dollars and bought her a statue of a saint. She beamed when we presented it to her. She cherished that statue for the rest of her life.

When she died, it felt like that Christmas but turned inside out. Instead of joy, we felt sorrow, and Richie and I were making the arrangements, planning the funeral, writing up the obituary. Our brothers and sister seemed to disappear. We were the youngest ones, the unwanted ones, who now clung to her the most tightly.

Nobody could ever replace her. Who could I go to after she was gone? Who could listen to me without judging? I needed her advice, support, solutions, and help. I was never more lost than after I lost my mother.

# CHAPTER FOURTEEN

My parents had been married for forty-five years. After my mother's death, my father seemed as lost as I was. He and my mother had always been gentle with each other, and even though I didn't always respect my father, I knew the love between my parents was real.

Every woman on my mother's side of the family, starting with my grandmother, had buried her husband. Everyone in my family assumed my father would die first. That was just how things worked. Besides, we joked, my father wouldn't know what to do on his own. That was the truth. My mother's death seemed to unhinge him. He wandered around in a kind of fugue state. I was too busy holding myself together to help make things better, but in spite of our history, I worried about him. The emptiness we both felt after my mother's death was the first thing we ever really had in common.

Two weeks after becoming a widower, my father announced that he was going to Puerto Rico to visit his brother. He said he needed time to reconnect with himself, to get reoriented. I agreed. My father needed to get away from that apartment, which in a way was really *her* territory. Dad considered himself the head of the family, but the household was always my mother's domain, and going home to that empty apartment wasn't doing my father any good. My father departed for Puerto Rico, and I got to work putting my life back together.

Things were a little rough with Tony before my mother's death, but after she passed, we patched things up. Her death came as a shock, and it made me cling that much more tightly to the few people in my life I truly loved. Tony always tried to spare me the details of what went on while he was in prison; this meant that during our visits and phone calls, I was usually unloading my baggage on him.

"I'm glad your father's going on this trip," he told me.

"Me, too," I said. "It'll be good for him to get some time to himself."

"It will be good for *you* not to have to go to that apartment every day to check up on him."

It was true. I needed to focus on the changes in my own life. Since my mother had always taken care of the kids, they went to the little school a few blocks from my mother's house so that she could walk to get them more easily. Now that I was on my own, I transferred them to a bigger school downtown, closer to where I worked. I'd lost all my mother's support, and I still had to sort out how I'd manage everything.

"I miss you," I told Tony. "I wish you were here."

"I wish I were, too," Tony said earnestly. "Since I'm not, please, make some time for yourself. Your father's going away to get out of his own head a little. You need to do the same thing."

"I'll do my best." I was always doing my best in those days.

I was lost for the two weeks my father was away. I resolved to work on my relationship with him once he got back. God knew we could both use some support. The day my father returned, Richie and I went to see him. We walked into the apartment, and something felt off. I expected to find my father still frayed at the edges, but he was surprisingly upbeat.

Maybe I should have been glad my father was happy, but it struck me as disrespectful. My parents had been married for the better part of fifty years. Shouldn't losing someone like that leave a lasting mark on his life? Shouldn't her death crush him for just a little while? My father did not seem crushed. His whole attitude had changed while visiting his brother.

"What's going on, Dad?" Richie asked, picking up on the vibe. "You seem…good."

"Better than good," our father said. "Actually I want to talk to you both about something, especially Carmen."

My brother and I glanced at each other. "OK," I said, "so let's talk."

"While I was staying with your uncle, I met some-one—his neighbor, a lovely woman. She's coming to visit me for a week, sometime very soon."

I was at a loss for words. My mother hadn't even been dead a month, and my father was already making new friends.

"Who is she?" Richie asked. I could tell he was try-ing to keep his cool, although his voice shook a little when he spoke.

"Like I said, a neighbor of your uncle's. Sweet girl."

"Girl?" I choked.

"She's twenty-seven," my father clarified.

"*I'm* twenty-seven!" I exclaimed.

"And Carmen's your youngest kid," Richie added.

My father held up his hands. "I know what you're thinking. You're worried I'll disrespect the memory of your mother."

"Of course you are!" I practically shouted.

"I've thought about that. See, I was thinking we could stay in a hotel instead of here. Then I thought to myself, '*Carmen has an apartment.* Why don't the two of us just trade for a week?'"

I was speechless with fury.

"What do you say?" my father asked. "Does that sound reasonable?"

The worst part of the conversation was that my father didn't seem the slightest bit sheepish or embarrassed. Richie had to drag me from the apartment to keep me from throttling our father. My promise to build a relationship with him went out the window. I'd been ready to try, but I no longer saw the point.

In the end, Dad and his girlfriend stayed in what I still always considered to be my mother's apartment for the weeklong visit. Richie, always the peacemaker, kept trying to put things right. "Everyone grieves differently, Carmen," he reminded me.

"Do you know how Dad paid for the ticket to Puerto Rico?" I demanded.

Richie shrugged uncomfortably.

"The life-insurance money from the life-insurance policy Mom left him. You remember Mom? She's been gone for less than a month, Richie. But here's Dad, with a girlfriend my age, and he asks to bring her into *my bed* because he doesn't want to disrespect Mom's memory. You don't think he already had that taken care of?" I was ranting, and I knew it. Dad gave me a way to channel all my helplessness, and the hollow feeling that was growing inside me when Mom died now turned to anger. I knew what I'd lost, but did Dad? Dad was spending my mother's life-insurance policy on a new fling.

"We always said we couldn't imagine Dad on his own," Richie reminded me. "This is his way of coping, I guess."

"It's disgusting," I said.

Even peacekeeper Richie didn't disagree.

Dad's Puerto Rican girlfriend visited twice, but I wasn't there to meet her. All my respect for my father was gone, and we'd never had a great relationship to begin with. Richie brought me updates from time to time. He and Dad were still close, since he was able to excuse my father's behavior. I couldn't.

When the money from the life-insurance policy was gone, the girlfriend disappeared, too. *Good*, I thought. *He deserves it.* Pretty soon after that, Dad was seeing another woman, this time someone from the building we'd lived in all those years. While she was alive, my mother had sometimes babysat this neighbor's granddaughter. The neighbor moved in with Dad and got rid of my mother's things.

My father never asked if we wanted to keep any of our mother's belongings. He had a new woman now, so it was time for the old stuff to go. Every time I thought about what my father was doing, I actually shook with rage. Tony could hear the fury in my voice when I told him that a friend of the family was trying to erase my mother by throwing away her possessions. "You know what human instinct tells me?" I asked. "All this is happening so fast. It makes me wonder if something happened between them…before."

Tony mulled this over. "Do you want me to punch your father in the face?"

In another life, I'd have told him yes. It was something I'd fantasized about lately. But Tony was actually capable of shooting someone, so I had no doubt that, if I asked, Tony would knock my father out on his first day as a free man. "No!" I cried. "No! Don't do it!" And for the first time in weeks, I laughed.

Months later, Richie bought a house. He was still trying to find a way to keep our family from falling apart, so he made my father an offer. Dad and his girlfriend could stay with him, but on the condition that I could have the old apartment. Much to my surprise, Dad agreed.

The apartment was much bigger than the one where I lived a few blocks away, and under normal circumstances I could not have afforded it. Because the apartment wasn't changing names, however, I would pay the same rent my parents had paid on their original lease. It was just $325 a month, which was less than what I was paying for an apartment half the size.

If Dad was worried that my mother's ghost would haunt the apartment and judge him for his transgressions, then I could only hope a part of her remained. She was gone, and I could never again turn to her for support, but her domain became mine. I ate in the same kitchen where she'd cooked so many meals for me and had offered me so much advice. Even after she was gone, my mother managed to provide for me.

# CHAPTER FIFTEEN

A cousin came to see me almost a year after my mother's passing. She was fifteen, just a kid, and not much older than my daughter. She'd been at the Fourth of July barbecue just before my mother's death, but I hadn't seen her much since then. She hugged me when I met her at the door, but she had trouble looking me in the eyes. Something was obviously wrong. "What's going on?" I asked. "You look like you've got something on your mind."

"I want to—I mean—I need to talk to somebody." She folded her arms and shook her head. "Maybe I shouldn't tell you. I don't know what to do."

"I've been there," I said, thinking of Cory. "You know you can trust me, right?"

She nodded, brushing hair away from her eyes. "Yeah, I guess. This is hard."

I thought of offering her a seat on the old white wicker lawn furniture that had accompanied me to my parents' apartment, but this conversation seemed to require a little more care. On impulse I brought her to the kitchen, the place where I'd always gone for my mother's advice. My young cousin sat at the table, running her hands over the scratched surface. It seemed she needed to move, to be doing something, as if she'd stall out if she sat still for too long.

"So?" I asked coaxingly. "What's the matter?"

"It's about your brother," she said.

"Which one?" More than ever, I'd thought of Richie as my only brother. He was the only one worth keeping around, anyway.

Instead, she named my oldest brother, and my throat closed up. "What happened?" I finally asked.

My cousin tilted her head to one side and then the other. Her mouth quivered, and tears built up in her eyes before spilling down her cheeks. I didn't push her. I just waited. "He…" she said at last. "I mean, he…" She wiped away the tears and managed to regain her composure. "He touched me."

I put my hand on hers to still her. She cried again. Slowly, piece by piece, she told me exactly what had happened. I didn't interrupt, but my heart grew heavier with every passing moment. "I'm so sorry, baby," I said when she was done.

"You believe me?" she asked softly.

"Of course I do." I paused. I'd never told anyone but Tony about what my brother did to me. "He did the same thing to me."

My cousin nearly folded in on herself then. She laid her arms on the table and let her head drop into them. "I'm sorry, too," she whispered. "I didn't know what you'd say to me."

I rubbed her back, feeling sick to my stomach. I was sick with my brother for being the kind of man who would do this. I was sick with myself for never having spoken up about what my brother did. I wondered if it would have stopped if I'd told someone. If people knew the truth about him, would they have kept their kids out of his reach?

"I'm glad you came to me," I said. "I'll do everything I can to make sure this doesn't happen again. I just wish I could have kept you safe."

She wiped her eyes. "What are you going to do?"

"I don't know yet. What I do know is that I'm going to tell everyone what a sick fu—" I cut myself off. "That is, what kind of person my brother is."

"They won't believe you," she told me.

I frowned. "Why do you think that?"

"Because they didn't believe me."

"Who didn't believe you?"

She twisted her hands together, looking like she might cry again. "I told my mother, and I told Annette."

"You told his wife?"

My cousin nodded.

"And they didn't believe you?"

"Well, maybe they did." She traced the marks on my table again. "But even if they did, they told me not to talk about it."

My hands tightened into fists. I felt the old anger, shame, and guilt all over again. I'd cried myself to sleep after what my brother did to me. No good had come from my silence. Instead, this girl I loved had suffered the same way I had.

"This ends here," I told her. "This ends with you. This ends with me."

I couldn't wait until the next time I saw Annette. I called her that night.

"Our cousin came by today," I told her, and I said the girl's name. "She told me an interesting story."

"Ah," said Annette "Yes, I think I've heard it before."

"I believe her."

My sister-in-law hesitated. "I believe her, too." I pulled the receiver away from my ear and stared at it, wondering if I'd misheard her. Her voice, tinny and distant, came through the phone as if she were talking to me from the other side of the world. "It's a terrible thing," she said. "I haven't been sure what to do."

*Leave him, maybe?* the voice in my head said, but instead I asked, "When did she tell you?"

"About a year ago."

I shook my head. "Annette, she told you a year ago, and you haven't done anything since then? You haven't said a word?"

"Of course I told someone," Annette snapped. "I told your mother. You don't think I live with the guilt every day?"

"When did you…" I suddenly remembered standing in my mother's kitchen the night of her heart attack and noticing the way Annette hung around and avoided my eyes. I now knew what had broken my mother's heart so badly that she hadn't fought to come back to us.

The Fourth of July holiday of 1995 was the first and last time my mother had all five of us kids in her apartment at once. We'd spread out across the country, and she was thrilled to gather us all up for a few days. Such a large reunion took a lot of coordination and planning. It probably would have been years before she'd have been able to get us all together in one room again, even if things had gone well.

When Annette told her about my brother, Mom must have known it would be the last time we'd all be together. She let herself go because she knew she couldn't fix us. That's what I believe in my heart.

Yes, my cousin had been molested, as had I. The truth, though, was that we'd all lost something. Mom was the glue that held us together; without her, the rest of us came unstuck. If she were still with us, then maybe I would have done things differently. Maybe I wouldn't have felt so angry or betrayed. But she was gone.

I told the truth, and I didn't stop. I waged total war on my brother. I told everyone in the family, and even friends of the family, about what my brother had done to my cousin and me. "You shouldn't talk about this," my aunt warned me.

"Why?" I demanded. "If we shut up, it won't just go away."

"Talking about it won't fix anything," she told me. "It will be hard on the family."

A lot of people felt that I was the problem, mostly because I was the one who refused to let it go. Maybe things would have been different if I'd simply shut my mouth. Maybe we all could have pretended to be happy and acted fine, and nothing would have changed. Maybe we could have learned to live with it. For me, though, the truth was too important and the lie too big to ignore. In fact, the lie was bigger than I knew.

True, some people warned me to back off, but others—among the younger generations of the family and even among our childhood friends—admitted that my brother had abused them, too. Every story horrified me. If I'd spoken up, could I have spared the next person? If they had spoken up, could they have spared my cousin?

When I was a little girl, I asked myself, *Why me*? Why did my brother invite *me* into his bedroom? Was there something about me that had made him single me out? Had I somehow brought it on myself? It could have been anyone. That's just who my brother was.

I'd like to think that my mother would have believed me if I'd gone to her when I was small. I feel every mother knows her child, and at least a small part of her must have suspected the truth. But would my mother have spoken out, or would she have shut herself off and just prayed for the problem to go away? Prayer isn't the same as action, and action was what I needed. Since I couldn't know what my mother would have done, I turned to my father. We'd hardly spoken since my mother's death, but I wanted to tell him what had happened.

I went to Richie's house, where my father and his girlfriend were living. Richie's house wasn't large, but it was comfortable, and my father and I settled in for the conversation I dreaded. He listened in silence while I told him what my brother had done to me, what he had done to my cousin, and what he had done to so many others over the years. I told him about my conversation with Annette and about Mom's heart attack.

When I was done, he shook his head. "This is all her fault," he told me. "That girl as good as killed your mother."

"That girl?" I demanded. "*That girl* isn't the one who broke her heart. My brother's the one you should blame."

"If she'd kept quiet, we could have gotten on with things."

"And nothing would have changed!"

"She talked, and look what happened. Your mother is dead."

I stood up, clenching my hands to keep myself from snatching something up from a shelf and throwing it across the room. I wanted to break something. I wanted to make a scene. I wanted him to understand how much this meant to me, but I finally understood that we never would see eye to eye. We didn't just think differently. We lived differently. "You know this is the end," I told him. "It's over. This family will never be the same."

"I know that," he snapped. "I hope you're happy."

I was nowhere near happy. I stormed out of my brother's house; the only emotion I felt besides anger was a little gratitude. I was glad I hadn't turned out like either of my parents in the end—neither submissive nor self-absorbed. I was glad I could fight for the truth, even if the truth had torn apart what was left of my family.

In the end, my brother and his wife moved to California. Even if the rest of my family didn't talk about the things he'd done, there was too much tension for them to stay. I was glad to see them go.

Even with my brother on the other side of the country, I felt I couldn't shake my anger. I probably would have gone crazy if it were not for two factors. First, my children were flourishing in their new school. Especially in Ellie, I could see hope for a future I'd never had, even considering how hard I'd worked and how far I'd come. My kids had real opportunities ahead of them, and I needed to make sure they had every chance of success.

Second, Tony was released from prison at last.

# CHAPTER SIXTEEN

Ever since Tony had first been sentenced, I'd hoped his good behavior would get him paroled early. That never happened. He was in prison for the full twelve years, and I got so used to living my life around his sentence that the idea of his coming home was almost unreal.

It was late December. It was cold and snowy, and Christmas was only a few days away. I had to pick Tony up and drive him back to the real world. He'd been moved a few times, each time a little closer to New York City, so the drive was now about four hours—still a long haul, but not nearly as long as the ten-hour drive I faced in the beginning.

Richie came with me to pick up my husband from prison. Richie was always there for me by taking the kids on trips and looking out for us. I think that by the time Tony was released, Richie saw his return as a release for himself, too. He would no longer have to worry so much about the kids and me. We had someone else to make sure we were OK.

I braced myself for the moment when Tony and I would meet outside a prison for the first time in over a decade. We'd had a taste of freedom in the prison trailers, but this was something different. I wasn't sure how to prepare, so by the time we reached the prison, I was feeling halfway anxious and halfway dreamy. None of it seemed real, as if I were just imagining that Tony was coming back to me the same way I'd imagined it happening so many times before.

But this was real. As we pulled up to the prison for the last time, I tried to take it all in—the joy, the relief, the satisfaction of knowing that what I'd waited twelve years for was finally happening.

When Tony walked out—in his own clothes, not the orange jumpsuit he always wore in the visiting room— I took a few hesitant steps toward him. *I wondered what I should say. What did he need to hear at that moment, which must have been an even bigger deal for him than for me? Before I could decide*, Richie had launched himself at my husband, practically jumping into his arms to give him a bear hug. When Tony finally pried him off, Richie was blubbering like a baby.

"Good Lord," I asked, "who are you happy for— Tony, me, or yourself?"

"Everybody," said Richie, wiping his face. "All of us."

Tony grinned and swept me up, crushing me to him with all the fierce love that had kept me waiting all these years. "At last," he murmured. I didn't say a word. I didn't have to.

As we began our walk toward the car, a correctional officer gave Tony a knowing look. "Ashe, I'll see you again," he said.

Tony looked back over his shoulder. "I don't know what you're talking about. I'm never coming back here. You won't see *me* again."

We got to the car, Tony gripping my hand so tightly my fingers went numb. Before we got in, Tony looked back at the building. He hadn't spent his whole sentence there, but it was a symbol of all that had gone wrong for us and all the lost time we had to make up for. He leaned in and kissed me. "Ma," he said, seriously, "never again. Never, ever again."

We rode home in silence. It wasn't the strained silence of people trying to figure out what to say next. Tony gazed out the window, watching the world roll by, and I could only imagine what it was like for him to finally be free. We had beautiful scenery for most of the drive, and then we hit the city. Home.

Tony just kept looking. Richie and I kept quiet. I wondered what he saw, how the city must have changed in twelve years. Everything changed so gradually day by day that I couldn't even remember what he'd missed. "No phone booths," he said suddenly. "There used to be phone booths on all the street corners. I haven't seen a single one."

"Well, you know, with cell phones..." Richie waved a hand dismissively.

"Cell phones?" Tony considered this. "They're like pagers, right?"

"Yeah," I said, "sort of. I'll show you."

Tony went back to watching. That was the first hint that we'd all have a lot of adjusting to do. For years I'd imagined Tony's release, but I'd missed a few key details in my daydreaming. I hadn't quite wrapped my head around how rough the early days of the transition would be for him. I hadn't been able to picture what it would look like for the rest of us, either.

We got home shortly before school let out, and the kids raced home to see their dad. They barreled into the apartment and jumped on him, as enthusiastic in greeting him as Richie had been.

When we sat down to eat dinner as a family that night, Tony pulled his plate close to his chest and rested his elbows on the table, surrounding the plate as if someone might snatch his food away. The kids exchanged looks. "What are you doing?" I asked. "You're acting like a crazy person."

Tony looked at me and then adjusted his arms so they rested on the table. Within a few minutes, however, he was back to slouching over his plate. The kids looked as if they might laugh, but I studied my husband carefully. He'd always spared me the details of what went on in prison. Maybe he was used to other prisoners trying to snatch food from his plate. I let it go, since this was only his first day back.

We slept together in our bed that night, and I sighed with contentment. Wasn't that one thing I missed the most—the closeness of him, his smell, the warmth of his body beside mine? True, he tossed and turned more than I remembered, but I reminded myself yet again that this was a big transition. *We'll work it out.*

In the middle of the night, Tony rocketed out of bed. I sat up, blinking into the darkness. His voice came from the hall. "What's going on?" he asked.

Ellie answered, sounding frightened. "I have to pee."

When Tony came back into the room, I asked, "What the hell?" In my sleepy state, I'd forgotten that I was trying not to judge his behavior too harshly.

"I heard something, but it's just Ellie. You can go back to sleep."

I rolled my eyes and flopped back on the bed. I would have loved to be able to go back to sleep, but my husband kept fidgeting in the bed and jumping at every noise from the street. It wasn't exactly the romantic and tender first night back I'd had in mind.

Over the course of the next few months, things got more and more tense, and I started to question my sanity. Tony was on edge all the time, which made the rest of us almost as jumpy as he was. The kids accosted me in the kitchen one day. "Mom," Little Tony asked, "is something wrong with Dad?"

"Wrong how?" I asked evasively.

"He flips out whenever we go to the bathroom at night," Ellie said.

"We have to tiptoe, and even then he sometimes hears us," Little Tony added.

"Plus he acts crazy at dinner," Ellie said.

"And he's so jumpy," Little Tony concluded, rounding out the evidence that their father had lost his mind.

I chose my words carefully. "It's hard for him right now. When he left, you two were babies. Now you're teenagers. Things have changed a lot, and your dad's been through a lot, too. He just needs to get a few things out of his system."

My kids both seemed skeptical, but they agreed to be patient with their dad. I didn't tell them how often I asked myself, *Did I really wait all this time for this crazy fool?*

In other ways, though, Tony's adjustment to the free world was seamless. He was released on the twenty-first of December, and he had a new job at the neighborhood barbershop by the twenty-third. The owner had known Tony years before, so the man took a chance on him.

He also got custody of his daughter Tracie. He never told me exactly what he'd said to her mother, but one day he went to see her, and that night Tracie came home with him. Tracie, too, was on edge a lot, since she had her own baggage. It was challenging for her to cope with Tony's behavior and share an apartment with two other kids. Tony compromised and settled her in with his mother. He could be in her life again, but she would have a little space of her own while everyone figured out their own personal issues. I wondered if Tracie felt as uprooted in those days as I did.

I'd heard that some people, after they got out of prison, spent a lot of time feeling bad for themselves and blaming their circumstances and experiences for what they'd done. Tony was never like that—which was good, because I wouldn't have tolerated that. He always acknowledged what he had done and took responsibility for his actions. That and his solid work ethic helped him settle into his new job with ease.

His parole officer was floored. "I wish every case was like yours," he told Tony.

"I want to integrate back into society," said Tony earnestly. "I don't want to relax and waste time. I've done enough of that."

Tony's boss didn't mind that the parole officer had to check on him at work. It was another matter for us when the officer had to check up on him at home. If we were out in the city, Tony would turn frantic. "We have to get back home in time!"

"No," I countered. "*You* have to get home in time. I have plans tonight, and they don't run on your parole schedule."

We had to get used to each other all over again in those first months. Tony's life wasn't the only one to have changed. I'd been raising two kids on one salary for over a decade, and Tony's return made things easier on that front. I'd also had the freedom to choose what I did with my spare time, and I didn't answer to anyone for my actions. My kids and I had a routine, and Tony threw things off by not knowing what we were supposed to do next or by asking questions instead of just doing what I told him to do.

Sometimes I had to catch myself from saying things like, "Don't ask questions. I've been doing things without you this whole time." I didn't want to go back to being on my own, but I'd forgotten how to be a team member rather than the team captain.

I always involved Tony in the kids' lives when he was away. I had them bring their report cards to the correctional facility and had them ask Tony's opinion about letting them go to parties or sleepovers. They were used to waiting for Daddy's permission. When he got out, they never disrespected him, because he'd always been a big part of their lives.

On top of that, they were scared to death of him. It's hard to sass someone when you don't dare make eye contact with him.

A few months into this new life, I went to my friend Ginger for advice. "Tony's driving me crazy," I told her. "I mean, we've always driven each other crazy, but this is different. When he was away, I could just hang up the phone or go home and put it behind me. We lived in two different realities. Now that we're in the same world again, I feel stuck. I feel like I threw away my twenties on a man I don't know anymore. What if things never go back to the way they were?"

Ginger's family was German and Italian. Maybe that was why she didn't have any interest in whining. She was always ready with the reality checks I'd always depended on my mother for, and this time was no exception. "You chose to wait for him," Ginger said. "You knew what you were doing. This is what you wanted, even if it doesn't look the way you thought it would."

I swallowed the rest of my complaints. She was right, of course. I wanted Tony's release to take me back in time, but we'd both changed a lot during our years apart. It wasn't fair to want the old Tony back any more than it would be fair for him to want the old Carmen back. We were new people, and this would only work if these new people could find a way to live and love together.

It took about six months for us to settle into a new rhythm. Tony stopped guarding his food and jumping at every noise, and I stopped making all the decisions about our daily routine. We learned to balance each other again.

The one thing Tony did leave to me was how we raised the kids. Ellie was the valedictorian at her high school, and Little Tony performed regularly with a large and well-known Harlem choir. Both kids got excellent grades, so I had no doubt they would both get into college.

One night as we got ready for bed, Tony told me, "I'll follow your lead with the kids. I'm just the enforcer. You've done a wonderful job."

"Thank you," I said. "They've stayed out of trouble. They're smart, and they're willing to work for what they want."

Tony considered this in silence for a while before getting into bed beside me and pulling me close. "A girl for you, a boy for me," he said. "I'm so glad you agreed to have Little Tony." Then he shook his head. "But you were right. Two are plenty. How did you manage them on your own? They have so much energy!"

"Practice," I said. "Balance. Compromise."

"That sounds about right." Tony switched off the light.

# CHAPTER SEVENTEEN

Finally, for the first time in years, we were building a nearly normal life. Instead of spending weekends in the state penitentiary, my family now got to spend time together doing ordinary things. Tracie visited us from time to time and gradually became more comfortable with the kids.. Her mother had told Tracie some horrible lies about me and about Tony as well. Once she saw that we were relatively ordinary, all things considered, she opened up a little bit.

The cousin who'd come to Annette and me about the abuse now spent much of her time with us, too. "You saved me, Carmen," she told me. "You were the only one who believed me." I welcomed her into our home with love and protection.

With all these extra people around, my parents' old apartment now felt a little cramped. I still thought of my mother every day, especially when I sat at her kitchen table or went into her old bedroom, which was now mine. But the rooms also reminded me of my father, my brother, and all the heartbreak that came with any interactions with my surviving family, apart from Richie. It was time to move on, so Tony and I bought a house and packed up our things.

Tony was doing so well at his job that before long he was able to open his own shop. He wanted to call the business R. A.W. Barbershop. The letters stood for *ready and willing*, which was always his attitude to chasing his dreams. We applied for a lease on a little space in Harlem. The landlords gave us a tour before he signed the lease, and Tony was practically bouncing off the walls. "It's perfect, Ma," he kept saying.

The landlord smiled generously. "We'll give you a chance to make it work," he said.

I rolled my eyes after we left. "*Give* us a chance, huh? Seems like we're paying for the chance, but he's right. You'll make it work. I know it."

"It's the American dream, right?" Tony said. "Our own house, our own business. Did you ever think we'd be here?"

I sized up my husband, the man I'd waited a dozen years for while he was in prison, the man who'd saved me from my stalker, the father of my children. "I always knew it," I told him. "We're at our best when we're together. You don't settle, and neither do I."

Tony kissed my cheek. "You know how to build a man up, don't you?"

"Tony," I said seriously, "if you were the kind of man who *talked* about all the things you were going to do, things would never work out with us. You see what you need to do, and you do it. That's one reason I'm so crazy for you."

"Crazy, huh?" He kissed me again.

Every summer, Tony's family threw a huge family reunion. Tony loved these get-togethers, but while he was away, I hadn't gone to any of them. For one, it was always a long drive. And what would I have said when I got there? It was his family. I could barely cope with my own family. They would have asked too many questions about my life, so to avoid that, I stopped going. Life without Tony was hard enough for my children and me without also having to act happy around Tony's family.

Now he insisted on going to every reunion. They always happened in September, but they were never in the same state from one year to the next. Tony's family had spread all over the country, so each year another section of the family played host. We'd driven to the Carolinas, Virginia, Florida, and sometimes even farther; the kids complained about the drive every year. "I don't want to go," Little Tony groaned.

"We always have fun when we get there," I pointed out.

Ellie rolled her eyes. "Yeah, after being in the car for about a million years."

I held up my hands. "If you hate it so much, then take it up with your father. I'm not getting involved." Family always mattered to my husband, and I wasn't about to get in the way of that.

The only time Ellie didn't make it to the reunion was during her first year of college. The reunion happened the same week as move-in day and orientation on campus. Tony grudgingly let her go, but the next year, he researched the timing to be sure that neither of the kids would ever miss the family reunion again.

Neither Tony nor I finished college. I took medical courses to become a technician in the radiology lab where I worked, but I'd never lived in a dorm or eaten in a dining hall. Since we had no idea what the college experience would be like, we overly prepared with Ellie. I wanted my daughter to have everything she needed. We bought her new sheets, new clothes, and even new textbooks from the campus bookstore. When the bill came in, I almost collapsed. The books alone cost almost $2,000.

Before the start of the next semester, Ellie called me. "I was talking to my roommate, and she says you can get used books through some of the bookstores."

"Do that!" I told her. "Who cares if they have high-lighter in them? That just means someone else thought that part was important."

The next year, we told her to take sheets from the closet. By the time Little Tony started college, we more or less dumped him off at the curb in front of his dorm. If he felt cheated by all the fuss we'd made over his sister's first year, he didn't complain. "Look at him," Tony said, waving good-bye. "Look at their lives. Look at our lives. Look what we were able to produce."

"See?" I said. "We did pretty well, considering."

"Are you kidding? We did great."

Tony's business took off, and with the kids in college now, we made some plans of our own. We visited Puerto Rico, and for the first time I got to see the place my parents had come from. It was the honeymoon Tony and I never had. We stood at the El Conquistador Resort and took in the green slopes, palm trees, and blue water that was so crystal clear we could see right down to the white-sand bottom.

During our vacation to Jamaica, the airport lost our luggage for a day, and our hotel was overbooked. As compensation, we were put up in a five-star resort, all expenses paid. The management strongly advised us not to leave the resort, but Tony ignored them. He wanted to see how Jamaican people actually lived, so we went out every day to explore the nearby town. I stood out, clearly an anxious tourist, but Tony blended in with the locals and made friends wherever we went. It reminded me of when we first moved in together, when he knew the name of every pimp and ho along our street. He was never quick to judge people, and that made everybody like him right away. I held his hand as he led me through the Jamaican streets and, despite all the warnings we'd heard at the resort, we felt as safe as ever.

Our trip to Mexico was different. We got scammed by a travel agency and were already at the airport before I realized that they'd taken our money without actually booking our trip. I reported the company to the police, and we ultimately got our money back, but our planned vacation was long over before we ever saw a dime.

"I'm still going to Mexico," I said, and Tony agreed.

We booked round-trip flights, but because we'd made last-minute plans, we couldn't get a direct flight back to New York and had to be routed through North Carolina. "Fine," Tony said. "We'll make it work."

It took us a few days to settle down and enjoy our vacation, but eventually we relaxed and let off some steam. We always managed to find an adventure, and the next trip was never the same as the last. I was glad we'd gone to Mexico despite the initial problems.

During our stopover in North Carolina on the way back, we had to go through security a second time, since we were transferring from an international flight. The Transportation Security Administration had randomly selected Tony, so I sat down to wait for him, annoyed by the seeming racism in what the TSA called a random search. It got worse. The background check turned up a fifteen-year-old arrest warrant for someone who had the same name as Tony. He was detained overnight.

"You should get on the flight," the TSA officer suggested. "Your luggage is on there, and who knows when you'll be able to go home after this?"

I planted my heels, still in the flip-flops I'd worn on vacation. "I'm not leaving my husband."

The officer shrugged, clearly disinterested. "Then you'll need to find a hotel and figure out what you're going to do."

I'd packed all my clothes in my checked bag, keeping the heavier and more fragile souvenirs in my carry-on luggage. It was pouring out, and I walked around outside the airport in search of a hotel that would keep me as close to my husband as possible. The bag was so heavy that by the time I found a room, I almost threw it away. The rain hid the fact that I was crying, but it also soaked my shorts and T-shirt. I was freezing.

I went up to my room and sat on the bed and cried. None of this seemed fair. Tony and I had been through enough. Why was this happening to us? I went to blow my nose, and when I looked in the bathroom mirror, something in my reflection reminded me a little bit of my mother. *What would she have to say about all this? She certainly wouldn't* have tolerated *my self-pity.* I'd been through a lot worse than this. I wasn't helpless, unless I let myself be.

I took a deep breath, got out my phone, and made calls to New York. I had to tell Pat that I would be a few days late. Then I tracked down documents to prove that the old arrest warrant wasn't for my husband. The agency I spoke to faxed these documents to my hotel, so I had everything in order for the next morning.

The paperwork cleared my husband, and his case was dismissed almost immediately. Tony and I left that courtroom so fast that any spectators might have thought it was on fire. We ran to the airport, made it through security without encountering any problems, and waited anxiously at the gate.

When our flight was called, Tony leaped to his feet and then sat down again. "Sorry," he said. "I don't want to draw attention to us, but…"

"I know," I said. "It's been…"

We stared at each other, at a loss for words to describe our miserable vacation. Finally Tony sighed. "I just want to get on the plane and get home," he said.

Every time a boarding section was called, Tony and I jumped and then sat down again when we learned it wasn't ours. Pretty soon we were giggling like a couple of kids. The people around us must have thought we were losing our minds. I was so relieved to finally be getting back to New York that I couldn't keep it in.

Years before, we'd walked into a courthouse with no idea of what we needed to get married. Now I knew where to call and what papers to track down to prove that my husband wasn't a wanted criminal.

"What would you do without me?" I asked as we boarded the plane at last.

Tony shrugged. "I dunno, Ma. And I don't want to know, either."

# CHAPTER EIGHTEEN

When Tony was in prison, I'd imagined what it would be like to have him back. If I'd overestimated how wonderful Tony's first few months back home would be, then I'd underestimated how content we would be years later after everything was finally under control. The kids were grown and taking care of themselves, we worked hard at jobs we enjoyed, we could afford vacations and put something aside, and we could let loose more than we ever had since the early days of our marriage.

Tony threw me a huge party for my fortieth birthday. He rented strobe lights and a red carpet and put on a real show. It reminded me of the way we'd lived when we were first married, back when we frequented the clubs. The party was adults only. Richie was the only person who was allowed to bring his children.

My kids were there, too, but they were no longer children by this point. Little Tony was halfway through college, and Ellie had been out of school for two years; she'd earned a degree in communications with a minor in business. I had big hopes for her future. She had a tremendous amount of opportunity ahead of her, and I couldn't wait to see how she'd make her mark on the world.

It was a fancy-dress party, sixties-themed in honor of the decade I was born. I brought several outfits and changed five times over the course of the night. It was that kind of party. Ellie wore a little gold dress that we'd found in the Village and a pair of Giuseppe heels. Partway through the night, Tony slouched over to me. "Have you seen what our daughter's wearing?" he demanded.

"I have. Isn't she beautiful?"

"She looks naked!"

"Oh, come on. She's stunning."

Tony glared across the room at Ellie, who was talking to her college sweetheart. She must have invited him. *Well, good for her.* She was in a class of her own, and I was glad she was enjoying my party as much as I was.

A few weeks later, Ellie came to me to tell me that she was pregnant. She'd gotten pregnant on the night of my birthday party. Tony's angst about her dress was nothing compared to my reaction to the news. I assumed she'd have kids someday—after she was married and was a few years into her career. It just didn't occur to me that she'd have kids so soon. I felt as if she'd thrown away everything I'd sacrificed for her. I didn't want her to have to struggle the way I did. I wanted more for her.

Part of me looked forward to meeting my first grandchild, but another part was angry at my daughter for settling down so early on. For five months, I couldn't bring myself to talk to Ellie. I didn't know how to be happy for her without also being disappointed over what I felt she'd thrown away.

My mother was the religious one in our family, and there was something she always said when she talked about God: "*Whenever you think you have a plan, he has another one.*" I told myself that this was God's plan, not mine. It didn't help.

I was completely out of control. I knew it, but I couldn't seem to shake my anger. Tony became my point of contact with Ellie. He took her out to breakfast, bought her clothes, planned her baby shower, and spoke with her every day. "I told Ellie to call," he said. "But she won't unless you talk to her first."

"Don't tell me what she's up to!" I snapped. "I don't want to hear it." Tony shrugged and let it go for a while.

The truth is that sometimes my anger and stubbornness made me want to punch myself in the face. I just couldn't understand why Ellie hadn't been more careful. Didn't she want a career? Didn't she care about her future as much as I did? I felt that I'd given up so much for her when we already had so little. I'd had her when I was young, so I knew how hard it was to balance a baby, the beginning of a career, and finances. I wanted her life to be easier than mine was. I wanted to protect her from hardship.

It was a good thing she had Tony to protect her from *me*. I wished I could just get past my frustration, but whenever I thought about how much I'd given up for my children, it hurt me to think that my daughter might have to make the same sacrifices.

A few weeks before the baby shower, Tony sat down on the couch and crossed his arms. "I've been planning this party for weeks," he informed me. "It's too much, and I need your help. It's time to cut the bullshit and move on."

I folded my arms and scowled at him.

Tony threw his hands in the air. "Ma, I've had to deal with your complaining and Ellie's pouting for months. Enough! You've got to be as sick of this as I am. What are you waiting for? What are you hoping she'll say? You might not be happy, but this is her life, not yours. Get over it."

"I'll talk to her," I said at last. Tony rarely ever pushed me, so I knew when he brought it up that he was serious. I wasn't winning this.

Ellie came over to our house, and I could tell she was as happy about the meeting as I was. It was the first time

I'd seen her since she'd told me of her pregnancy, and I found myself frowning at her belly. I thought, *What's happened to my little girl?* I wanted her life to be easy. I couldn't see how things could possibly be easy for her now.

Tony left Ellie in the living room with me. "Make nice, girls," he said, heading off to another part of the house.

Ellie waited.

"I'm sorry," I said. The words sounded a little lame, so I went on. "I wanted so much for you. I'm worried you'll put your life on hold now...and your career."

"OK," she said.

I took a deep breath. "I want you to know that I'm here for you no matter what."

"Even when you don't support what I'm doing?"

"Even when I don't *like* what you're doing," I said, correcting her. "I will support you, though. I just want you to be happy. I want us all to be happy."

She rubbed her belly. "I want to be happy, too," she said. "I just don't know why you're so much harder on me than you are on Little Tony."

*Because he's not the one who got pregnant,* I didn't say. "It's because I still see him as my baby. You—you're older. You're more grown up. You've always seen more of what was happening, and I know you're capable of so much."

"This is still my life," she pointed out.

I nodded, swallowing just enough of my pride to get the next words out. "I know, which is why I wanted to apologize."

Ellie hugged me. "All right," she said. "I'm not sure we're OK yet, but we will be."

The baby shower was enormous. Tony's plans didn't include a cake, and I came in to the picture too late to order one. For all that, the shower was almost as much of a production as my fortieth birthday had been. The rented hall listed a capacity of 125 people, but Tony had invited more than twice that many. "Who are they?" I asked Tony as he greeted yet another group of guests I didn't know.

"Clients from the shop," he said. "I've been telling everyone who comes in about my grandchild." He beamed at Ellie.

I rolled my eyes. "They've brought enough Pampers to last until the baby's two."

"Oh, don't be like that, Ma." He pulled me close. "This is my chance to get things right."

I squinted at him, opening my mouth to ask what he meant, but then I got it. He'd missed out on raising the kids and being part of their everyday lives. Instead, he could be there for this baby and make up for everything. I'd still been hanging on to some disappointment about Ellie's life, but I let it go right then. Everyone in my family was happy about this change, and I was going to be happy, too.

Tony stuck close to Ellie during the rest of her pregnancy. Anytime she needed something, he came to the rescue. Our daughter did not have to buy a thing. Even the baby's father didn't have to do anything. I think he was afraid to. Tony was totally absorbed in our daughter and the coming grandchild.

When our granddaughter Nyla was born, I was in the room with Ellie. The two Tonys waited for us in the next room, anxious to meet the newest member of the family. Despite my mixed feelings about her birth, I fell in love with our granddaughter from the moment I saw her. Nyla was the best birthday present I received that year or any other.

# CHAPTER NINETEEN

Around the time Nyla was born, we heard rumors at work. The partnership that had founded the Imaging Center was dissolving, and a new board was taking over. Pat had worked at the Imaging Center since its founding in the 1970s. She counted the doctors as close friends, almost a second family, and she'd made it clear early on that she would retire as soon as the practice changed hands.

Pat broke my heart when she told me she was leaving. She was more than just my boss. She had become family. I'm stubborn by nature and had a lot of anger in me then, but above all, I was loyal. Pat had taken a chance in hiring me, and I'd done my best to make sure she felt that the risk was worth it. I couldn't imagine staying at that job without Pat around. "If you won't be here, I won't be here," I told her. "I'll get another job."

Pat sighed. "Do the right thing for your family, Carmen. I'll worry about me. I don't want to have to worry about you, too."

"I can get another job easily," I assured her. "It won't be the same here without you."

"With you in charge?" she asked, grinning. "I'm sure it will be fine."

"Me?" I was taken aback.

"I recommended you for practice manager," she told me. "They need someone who knows what's going on to help ease the transition. Trust me. You can do this job with your eyes closed." I was deeply moved by Pat's words. She wasn't a woman who would recommend me for a job if she didn't believe I could do it, no matter how much she cared about me.

When Pat left later that year, I stepped into my new role with surprising ease. She was right. I could have done it blindfolded. I liked the work, and I was good at it.

Between my new job and Tony's business, things were looking stable. I could see the future coming our way, and it was bright. And didn't we deserve it? Things hadn't been easy for us, but we were fighters by nature. We'd earned some happiness.

At first I enjoyed the new position. I knew the office routines, I knew most of the patients, and I was adaptable enough to figure out how to handle a crisis on short notice. Most important, I knew all the staff; in the years I'd worked with everyone there, we'd built up a lot of trust. The staff respected me, but they were comfortable about coming to me with questions and complaints. It was perfect. Or so I thought.

Once the new partners got to know everyone, they started to look for ways to cut costs. The company started to lay people off, and I was frequently involved in the process. One day the new owners called me into a meeting and told me that they wanted to cut back on the budget by firing three senior staff members.

"Which three?" I asked, feeling a little sick to my stomach.

"It doesn't matter," they told me. "It's a budget issue, not a performance one. You know the staff pretty well. You pick."

I indeed knew the senior staff very well. These were people I'd worked with for fifteen years by this point. "How much money are you trying to cut?" I asked.

They gave me a number, and I went back to my desk. I couldn't imagine how I would possibly decide who to fire. I went over the numbers and tried to find even one employee who really deserved to be cut, but I couldn't think of a good reason to let anyone go. Like management told me, this choice was about money, not people.

I called a meeting with all twelve senior staff members. I explained the situation and saw the fear in everyone's eyes. I knew who had student loans to re-pay, who had a mortgage, who was going through a divorce, and whose kids were newlyweds. One of the staff asked, "So who's going?"

I shook my head. "Nobody."

One woman raised her eyebrows. "How will you ex-plain that to the owners?"

"We're going to take pay cuts—all of us." I sat up even straighter. "I realize nobody wants to do with less, but if we don't, three people will lose their livelihoods."

"Everyone?" she asked.

"Me, too," I said. "We're like family here."

We all agreed, even though some were happier about this arrangement than others. I didn't care. I did what I would be able to sleep with, even if it cost me part of my salary.

When, a few months later, I found my workload gradu-ally being reduced task by task, I knew the writing was on the wall. The company cut back my duties, and staff members stopped reporting to me. Everybody knew what it meant, and I was furious.

"After all this, they want to get rid of me," I told Tony. "I've worked there for almost two decades. I've held three positions. I should just walk out one day and not go back."

"Don't do that," he said. "If you walk, you get nothing. Make them force you to leave. Stay until they have to drag you out."

I scowled at him. "And then what? Do I just go out looking for more of the same? If a place I've dedicated my life to is willing to treat me like this, then—"

"So stay home."

I blinked. "What are you talking about?"

"You've worked hard," said Tony. "The kids are done with school, we've got some money in the bank, and the business is great. Stay until they offer you unemployment, and then take some time to figure out the next step."

I considered this. I'd had a job ever since I was a teenager, and I was something of a workaholic. Even after Tony was back in my life, I worked twelve to fourteen hours a day, six or even seven days a week. When I had Ellie, I worked until two days before she was born and was back in the office by the time she was a month old. It was pretty much the same with Little Tony. I couldn't imagine what I would do without a job. Stay home and be a housewife? That didn't sound like me.

A long time before this happened at work, I'd toyed with the idea of writing a book. I could give that a try, I thought. If that didn't work, then maybe I could do what Tony had done and become self-employed. I'd given a lot of my time and energy to a business that wasn't mine. What could I do if I put all that energy into my own interests? "I'll think about it," I said at last.

"We'd have to cut costs. And no more vacations for a while."

"So we'll stay here. We'll drop the life-insurance policies for now. If you could do some cooking, we could save some money there. We'll have to watch the electric bill and take the train more often instead of driving the truck. We can make it work."

It sounded reasonable to me. I wrinkled my nose. "You know how I feel about cooking," I said.

"You know how I feel about the train," Tony answered coolly.

The idea of taking some time off without worrying about money was sounding pretty good to me. In any event, the job was on the way out regardless of what I wanted. It was up to me to figure out how to be happy with whatever came next.

I lingered for weeks, taking some of my things home every night until my desk was clear. For the last month or so, I just went to work and played games on my computer. I wasn't ignoring my work, because there was nothing for me to do. The company no longer gave me responsibilities, but they also hadn't kicked me out yet.

At last I got a call on my phone line. The secretary on the other end sounded uncomfortable. "Hello, Carmen," she said. "There's a meeting at five o'clock this evening."

"That's a little late," I said mildly. "I have some-where to be after work."

"It's a mandatory meeting," she told me.

I smiled grimly. I knew the routine. "Can we have it a little earlier then?"

She cleared her throat. I knew management liked to do their firing at the end of the day, when most of the staff had already left.

"How about two o'clock?" I suggested. "If that isn't inconvenient."

"Not at all," she said, sounding strained.

They probably expected me to make a fuss, but I didn't. I knew they were going to ask me to leave, and I wanted to go on my own terms. I was quite matter-of-fact about the whole process.

The only things still remaining at my desk were my coat and my bag. I'd also printed off copies of a short thank-you letter, which I handed out to every-one on my way out the door. I wished them luck. I didn't look back as I stepped out into the street. I was done with business loyalty. It was time to rein-vent myself.

Being unemployed was strange for me. I was used to moving, to doing something every hour of the day. The first day I stayed home, I wandered around my house, paying attention to all the things I'd never looked at too closely before. The place was *dirty*. It was time to power clean.

When Tony got home, he reeled at the smell of bleach and, even more surprisingly, at the smell of dinner in the oven. I greeted him with a kiss, and he narrowed his eyes at me. "What have you done with my wife?" he demanded.

"I'm not done," I assured him. "There's lots more to do."

Tony nodded. "OK, this is a transition. I can see that."

When Tony came back from prison, he'd needed time to adjust to the real world. Maybe he knew what he was talking about. Maybe once I got used to unemployment, I wouldn't be so frantic. If so, it was going to be a long transition. By the end of the month, I was driving my husband crazy. Returning home to an ever-cleaner house, Tony would wrinkle his nose. "Does the house smell like bleach again? Surgeons could operate in here. Ma, I think we have to find you another job."

I had other reasons for enjoying the free time, though. That spring, Tony's grandmother had her ninetieth birthday, so we threw a huge party for her. Several family members had surgery and needed help once they were sent home, so I was able to be involved in all that, too. And I got to try my hand at writing in my spare time. I felt closer to my extended family and more connected to myself than I had in years.

In May, Tony and I celebrated our twenty-fifth-year wedding anniversary. Father's Day and his birthday were only a few weeks later, and we decided to do something special to celebrate. We planned to go horseback riding, but Tony changed his mind. "I don't feel up to it," he told me. "Let's do something low-key, just the two of us."

"Low-key? Like what?" I asked.

"Like…" He hesitated and then grinned. "Let's get manicures."

"Are you serious?" I pretended to check him for a fever.

"Sure, mani-pedis. What do you say?"

"I say you're the strangest man I've ever met."

He said teasingly, "It'll keep you from sanitizing the house today."

As I sat in the chair beside my husband while a clearly amused manicurist did his nails, I thought about how grateful I was. He glanced over at me, and we spoke to each other without saying words. He was as grateful as I was; the love between us ran both ways. True, we sometimes wanted to throttle each other now that I was spending so much time at home, but we always reconciled after we fought. We knew how to handle each other. The people who find that kind of love are blessed.

I was lucky. We were lucky. If we stayed lucky, we'd spend the rest of our lives together. Whenever you think you have a plan, another one's always on the way.

# CHAPTER TWENTY

I n June, Tony and I decided that I should look for a part-time job. I wasn't ready to go back to a nine-to-five position, and I was no longer sure about what sort of work I wanted to do. I was ready to reinvent myself, but I hadn't quite figured out what that looked like.

It began with TV's true-crime series *Snapped*. Tony left for work one day while I was watching a *Snapped* marathon. When he came back, I was sitting in the exact spot where he had left me. He stood there for a few moments, arms folded. "Is this reality TV?"

I nodded, still staring at the screen and riveted by the story. "It's about women who snap and commit horrible crimes."

Tony shook his head. "Well, you'd better snap back to reality, Ma. No more shows about killing your husband. We need to find you a job. Something

192

you like, OK? Something that will get you out of the house."

I went on a series of interviews, some more promising than others, but I didn't find a real fit. On June 27, 2012, I had an interview that sounded really interesting. I rode downtown with Tony on his way to work, planning to get my hair and nails done and to make a really good impression. I stopped by Tony's shop before the interview to show off my new look. "Wish me luck!" I told him.

He smiled and kissed my cheek. "Good luck."

"I'll call after I'm done and tell you how it went," I said.

"I look forward to it." Tony scooted me out the door.

The interview went wonderfully. As soon as I got out, I called Tony to say so. My call went to voice mail, but nothing was strange about that. I assumed he had a client, so I headed uptown and called again as soon as I got off the train. Again he didn't answer, and I frowned at my phone. Just as I hung up, my phone rang. It was my cousin, and I told her about the interview. "If you're free," she said, "we should celebrate with a drink." I thought about stopping by to tell Tony where I was going, but since he was too busy to answer my call, I decided not to interrupt.

Shortly after we met up, my cousin's phone buzzed. She read the text and frowned. "Has Ellie been calling you?" she asked. "She says she needs to talk to you."

I looked at my phone and was a little embarrassed to see that I'd missed a few calls from my daughter. I called back, and Ellie picked up on the second ring. "I can't find Daddy," she said at once. "He's not answering his phone."

"I wasn't answering my phone, either," I pointed out. "Little Tony works right across the street. Call and see if he can check in."

"I already did," said Ellie, sounding annoyed. "They told him Daddy left a few hours ago to go to the doctor's because he wasn't feeling well."

I frowned. My husband wasn't one to complain, so if he was going to see a doctor, something was definitely wrong. "We'll check it out," I promised. "We'll call the doctor. I'll go to the shop now." I hung up my phone and grabbed my bag. "Sorry, family emergency. I'll call you later."

"Good luck," my cousin said. "I hope it's nothing serious."

"I'm sure it's not. I'll call you when we have it sorted out."

The next few hours became a furious game of phone tag. My son called the doctor's office, and the secretary told us Tony had come and gone. I stopped by the shop and was alarmed to find that nobody there had seen Tony in hours. It wasn't like him to leave the shop like that, and I was even more disconcerted to find our truck still parked around the corner.

Little Tony called the surrounding hospitals. One hospital had admitted a man by a similar name, but it turned out to be someone else. In a panic, Ellie went to the police precinct to find out if Tony had been arrested. When they told her no, she broke down in the lobby, half from relief and half from frustration that we still didn't know where he was.

Not sure where else to call, I drove the truck home. When I arrived, all the lights in the house were on. The doors were unlocked, and Tony's cell phone was on the kitchen counter. It was obvious that my husband had been there recently. I called the kids to let them know. "At least it sounds like he left on his own," said Little Tony. "He must have been really sick. I'll call every hospital in the city if I have to."

We made a list of hospitals we hadn't tried and split them up between us. One of my calls finally turned up Tony's name in a patient registry; they told me that my husband had been admitted a few hours earlier. I waited for the kids to arrive and then drove all three of us to the hospital.

While I parked, Ellie and Little Tony ran in to find their father. I walked a little more slowly, wondering why he hadn't called me in all this time. *What if something horrible has happened to him?* To my surprise, Tony seemed fine. Ellie was crying again, and Little Tony seemed exhausted. He was drained from the search, and now that we'd tracked his father down, he was wrung out.

"Daddy was asking for you," he told me.

I sat on the edge of my husband's hospital bed. "What's the matter?" I asked.

Tony wasn't a complainer, and I could tell from his expression that something wasn't right. "I'm in a lot of pain," he said. "I'm not sure what's wrong."

"Well, I'm here now," I told him. "We'll sort this out."

While we waited for the doctor, two men waved Ellie over to a neighboring bed. They were obviously a couple. Both men showed Ellie a piece of paper. "What was that?" I asked when she came back over.

"Dad was screaming for you earlier," she said. "He gave them your number, but they couldn't reach you. He was off by one digit."

I was grateful they'd tried to help, but I hated the thought of my husband alone, screaming for me, in pain, and me not being able to help.

❦

"It was food poisoning," the doctor assured us. Ellie narrowed her eyes. She was a health nut, always keeping after her father to eat right, especially since he had high blood pressure. The doctor said, "We think it was the bologna sandwich."

"Oh my God, Daddy!" Ellie cried. "You know better!"

Tony looked chagrined. "I promise, I'll never eat another one."

The doctor cut in. "He threw it up earlier, and we've got him on a morphine drip for the pain, but we're just monitoring him. We want to observe him through tomorrow morning, and then he should be good to go."

I thanked the doctor for his time, and the three of us sat down to wait out the night with Tony.

Partway through the evening, a hospital aide came in to make sure nobody's sheets needed changing. She was a short, dark-skinned Hispanic woman, and she seemed to take a special interest in Tony. "If you need anything," she said, "just ask for Paula."

I felt my heart skip a beat. "Paula was Grandma's name," Ellie whispered. I nodded. It wasn't just her name—she had the same stature as my mother, too, and the same dark skin. It felt, in that moment, that everything was going to be fine. My mother's spirit was watching out for Tony. We were safe.

Around one in the morning, I told the kids to go home. Ellie kept rubbing her eyes, and if Little Tony yawned any wider, his jaw was going to pop. "I'm going back to the house," Little Tony said at last. "Call me if you need anything."

"You should both go," I said.

"I'll stay," Ellie said, insistent.

I shook my head. "It's OK. We'll figure out what the pain's all about."

Ellie opened her mouth to protest, but it turned into a yawn. "OK," she conceded. "I'll come back in the morning to get you two."

Little Tony cut in. "Ma, you look tired. Go home."

I took Tony's hand, and he squeezed it. "I'm not leaving my husband," I said. I kept thinking of my mother. I had refused to leave her, too. Maybe this time I could actually keep my loved one safe.

When the kids were gone, I lay my head down on Tony's bed and listened to his heavy breathing.

Sometime early in the morning, Tony woke me up.

"There's something wrong, Ma. I'm not..." His voice was shaky. I'd never seen my husband so rattled, even in the correctional facilities.

"We'll call a nurse." I reached over to push the button to alert the nurses. "We'll get to the bottom of this. You'll be fine, baby." Tony's face relaxed, and I leaned across the bed to kiss him on the lips.

I can never forget that—his anxiety, my promising he would be fine, the kiss.

The nurse on duty came by a minute or so later. She checked his morphine drip and frowned. "If it's just his stomach, the drip should still help with the pain." Shaking her head, she placed her fingertips on his wrist to check his pulse. Her lips pulled into a thin line. "I think your husband is having a heart attack."

"It was just a sandwich," I said, as though that could stop what was happening. Tony's blood pressure was usually high, and the pain from the food poisoning must have been a tremendous strain on his body and heart, but I wasn't thinking clearly enough to put those factors together.

More people appeared, summoned by the nurse, but I couldn't make sense of what they were saying. I watched, paralyzed, as they decided what to do next. If they had a plan for how to save my husband, then I wasn't listening. I clung to him until someone pulled our hands apart, and they wheeled Tony down the hall.

Yesterday I was worried about a job interview. Now we were in the hospital, my husband's life in danger, and I was helpless. I could do nothing but chase after his gurney as they rolled him away.

In a daze, I called Ellie. "Daddy's had a heart attack," I told her. I could tell my voice was hollow, but the sight of my husband being rushed away for emergency treatment was too much. "Get Little Tony and come here right away."

Ellie called back a few minutes later. "I can't reach him. I'll head your way, OK?"

As soon as we hung up, I called one of my neighbors. "Could you go to my house and make sure my son wakes up? Kick down the door if you have to. I need him here."

I fumbled with my phone. Everything had seemed fine up until a few minutes ago, and suddenly things

were serious. There were people I should call, I supposed, but it was hard for me to think. I dialed familiar numbers: Tony's grandmother, Ginger, Richie.

My kids arrived just as I'd hung up with my brother. "What's going on?" Little Tony asked. "What did
they tell you?"

"He had a heart attack a little while ago," I said. "I
haven't heard anything since."

Little Tony lifted his chin toward the man coming
down the hall behind me. I turned to see the doctor
I'd spoken to earlier. He placed a hand on my shoulder. "Don't touch my mother," Ellie said, suddenly defensive. "What you need to do is save my dad. Is he OK?
What's happening?"

"We're doing everything we can," the doctor promised. My detached brain couldn't make sense of the
seriousness in his expression.

Everything happened quickly around me; I was
stuck watching it all unfold but wasn't really part of the
activity. I kept thinking of my mother and how I hadn't
been able to protect her. *Where is Tony?* What was happening to him? He needed me, but they wouldn't let
me see him.

We gathered in the waiting room. Richie was there,
and we wondered when Ginger would arrive. The doctor returned, his face very grim. "I'm sorry," he said. "I
couldn't save him."

I stood still, doing everything I could to hold myself
together. Surely there was some mistake, some way to

take things back. None of this made sense. I watched my kids break down. Little Tony sank to his knees, and Ellie bent down over him to hold him close, and they just clung to each other while they cried and their noses ran. I couldn't move. I couldn't do anything. I had nothing to give them.

Ginger walked in and immediately took in the scene, understanding without being told. She put her arms around me, but I couldn't feel her there. I was numb.

Tony was gone. He had just turned forty-nine ten days earlier. There was no warning. Nothing leading up to that day prepared me for life without him. I've always been a spiritual person, and I believe everything in our lives happens for a reason. I believe my mother died because she knew, after her conversation with her daughter-in-law, that our family could never be whole again. I think that knowledge killed her.

With Tony, I couldn't see anything like that. I couldn't see why I had to lose him or why he had to leave. When he went, he took part of me with him. Through everything else, I'd managed to hold myself together, but he was gone now. For the first time, I cracked open.

# CHAPTER TWENTY-ONE

I had never really grieved for my mother, because her death had left me so angry. I'd had too much family drama to deal with and too many other people relying on me—the kids, Tony, my young cousin. I'd had to keep moving if I wanted to keep my kids fed, and anger was my coping mechanism. I'd had plenty of people to be mad at, with my father going off the deep end and my oldest brother's perversions coming to light.

After Tony's death, I felt only grief. The kids were grown up now and living on their own. Nobody depended on me and I had nobody to blame. In a way, anger had been easier for me to cope with than this. Anger kept me fighting. Tony's death took the fight right out of me. I was forty-five and didn't know how to be a widow.

As part of our plan to cut costs, Tony and I had canceled our life-insurance policies. Without Tony's income, I really needed a job. Frankly, though, who cared? I was empty. I was gutted. My husband had died on an operating table for no good reason. Money was the least of my problems.

For the second time in my life, I found myself in an empty bed, waking up to an empty refrigerator. When I'd been more or less a single mom, I'd worked hard to make sure my kids had what they needed. My kids were on their own now, and I had no one left to fight for except myself. Some days I didn't see the point.

I put what little energy I had into applying for jobs. The Internet company cut off my service every other month, which made it difficult for me to send in applications. Although I had paid a lot of my bills when I learned that I was being laid off, I still had some outstanding balances. I struggled to cover the most important bills first. The credit card bills had piled up, and I had no way to pay the mortgage.

I'd wanted a different life, but not this one—anything but this one.

For the most part, whenever collectors called, they were very understanding and willing to work with me to find ways of managing my debt. They didn't all get it, though. One man who called to collect on the truck payments asked, "Why don't you borrow some money?"

"I can't repay a loan right now, especially not with interest." This was the nice way of answering such an ignorant question.

"Can't your family or friends lend you anything?"

I laughed bitterly. "If they could, I'd spend it on food, not truck payments. My refrigerator is empty right now. Come see it if you want some proof."

The man hemmed and hawed and finally backed off. A little while later, I spoke to an equally clueless woman. "If you can't pay your bill by the end of the week, terrible things will happen," she warned me.

I laughed, and it was not a pretty sound. "One of the worst things that could happen to me just did," I informed her. "Now stop calling me, because I really don't have the money to pay you."

The kids wanted to keep the barbershop. I didn't see how we could afford to or who would have time to run it. I certainly wasn't qualified. I knew a little bit about what was involved, but the everyday details were beyond me.

Before long, the employees banded together. I didn't know everyone that well, but they wanted to be rid of us. They wanted to keep the shop running and force us out. I had very little fight left in me and few reasons to cling to that place. For the kids, keeping the shop was like saving one last piece of their father. For me, it was a reminder of what I'd lost.

In the end, we lost the shop. If I felt the employees had betrayed me, then that feeling was overwhelmed by the sense of inevitability that followed. I hadn't been able to keep Tony, had I? The shop was just another part of that.

Tony's death sucked the energy out of me, but it had the opposite effect on my children. They became eaten up with anger. Ellie, always sweet even when we fought, closed up. She transformed overnight from a soft-spoken and happy girl into a curt and assertive woman. She snapped at anyone for the slightest offense and turned every conversation we had into an argument.

For the first time in his life, Little Tony was the only man in the family now. When Tony had been in prison, I managed to make him part of our everyday lives. Now the balance was off, and I thought Little Tony was going to lose his mind. He bleached his hair. He got a nose ring. He did everything he could to set me off and pushed every one of my buttons. It seemed to me that both kids were trying to self-destruct.

The old me would have gone berserk, and Tony would have enforced some better behavior in them. The new me didn't even tell them off. We were all hurting from Tony's death, and I didn't have any anger left in me. When the kids attacked each other or me, I let it go. We were all in so much pain that I was sure we'd blow ourselves apart if we fought. We'd lose everything. I'd watched that happen after my mother's death, and I wouldn't risk losing my children.

Ellie wanted me to defend myself against her pain, , but I just let them hit without striking back. "When my father died, you died too," she told me. She wasn't wrong. I felt dead. I wasn't who I had been before. Tony's absence was a hole I kept falling into. The loss was like having a piece cut out of me, and I didn't know how to fill it.

# CHAPTER TWENTY-TWO

I was becoming desperate for work. Although I had gone on a number of interviews, nothing had come of any of them. I needed an income. I couldn't support myself on unemployment, and I didn't have the energy to learn a whole new trade. I had to ask my friend Marcia for help.

Marcia passed my résumé on to the HR department at her job, and within two days of the interview, they offered me a position as a data analyst. The pay was reasonable, but the idea of sitting in a cubicle all day didn't thrill me. I liked management, and I was good at it, but I wasn't enough of a fool to turn down a perfectly good job just because it wasn't my dream position.

The hiring process was lengthy, and in the interim I received an offer from another office. It was in radiology and was much more similar to the position I'd held before. I wasn't sure what to do. The idea of working as a data analyst didn't appeal to me, but I was grateful for the job offer. My friend had referred me, so I was reluctant to do anything that might bring her good word under scrutiny. I called her for advice. "Honey, if you want the other job, take the other job!" Marcia said.

"I don't want my backing out to reflect poorly on you," I told her.

"I only passed your résumé on. They hired you on your own merit."

"Are you sure it's OK?"

She laughed. "Don't worry about this, really. Do what's best for you."

I thought this over. I accepted the second position. It felt right, and in the end, that was what I needed— the right feeling. God knows I needed something to feel right.

To honor Marcia's recommendation, I decided to go back in person to thank the owners of that business for offering me a position. I wanted to make sure Marcia's reputation wasn't compromised in any way. The bosses were surprised I took the time to come in person, and they thanked me for it. "This is why we wanted you," one of the women told me. "Because this is the kind of person you are. Good luck, Carmen."

In the midst of chaos, the sun was shining on me just a little.

❧

I started my new position in mid-October, roughly four months after Tony's death. I worked hard, the way I always had. Sometimes I cried at my desk; the kids often called to check on me, which only made me cry harder. The staff and those above me never questioned this behavior, since my work was excellent. Everyone probably thought I was crazy, but they respected my privacy. The owners in particular were very understanding and sympathetic of my situation, and I was grateful for that.

Holidays were the worst. Thanksgiving, then Christmas, then New Year's—the holidays were meant to be a time for family, but my family was cracked wide open. My children were hurting just as much as I was, but for the first time, I could only carry myself. I felt like I'd lost my limbs. For that first year, I wore sunglasses all the time. Even at night, I didn't want anyone to see the pain in my eyes.

Thank God for my children. They kept me going. I couldn't imagine giving them any more pain, so I did what I had to do and kept moving.

Three months into my new job, I received a call back for a position I'd applied for when I first sent out applications. The woman on the phone sounded warm and enthusiastic. "We're looking for someone who can run the practice and oversee our hundred-plus employees. You seem like a great fit. Can you come in for an interview?"

I was thrilled. This was exactly the sort of job I was qualified for, and I would be working under two well-known physicians. The position seemed to fit me perfectly. I met with at least seven people on four interviews and was ultimately offered the job.

I felt bad about giving my notice over the holidays. I didn't want to taint my boss's vacation, but I also wanted to give the company plenty of time to find a replacement before I left. I asked to have a meeting on the second of January. At first the owners spoke to me, explaining all the changes they wanted to make in the coming year. I sat in silence, feeling more and more uncomfortable.

When it was my turn to speak, I hesitated. "I've been offered another job," I said at last. "I'm sorry it's so soon, but I have to do what's best for my family, and this is a tremendous position."

My boss nodded. "OK, what are they paying you? I'm going to make you a counteroffer."

I was surprised and taken aback by this. It had not occurred to me that my boss would do such a thing. I outlined the details of the position and nearly broke down when the owners came back with another offer. It wasn't about the money. The validation I felt over my bosses wanting to hang on to me was amazing. For months I'd dragged myself through life, but someone was noticing how hard I worked, and it wasn't even someone who cared about me particularly. If the owners of the practice were willing to fight to keep me, then it was because they thought I was an exemplary employee.

I called the other prospective employer back and thanked the woman for the job offer. "I've decided to stay in my current position," I told her. "The job sounds amazing, but it might be too much for me right now, given what's going on in my personal life."

"I can make a second offer," she said. "You made a great impression here. The doctors really want you." My soul and spirit needed that recognition. In the end, though, I had made my decision.

It felt good to be wanted, but it also felt good to belong somewhere. I dug my heels in and made myself at home. Ultimately, it was the best decision I could've made. The other job would have been challenging, and at another time that might have appealed to me. But at that point, I didn't have the energy to take on more challenges.

The job I kept was second nature to me. The work was almost reflexive, which meant that I could have done it in my sleep while still impressing my new bosses with my efficiency and precision. Best of all, my new coworkers and bosses respected my privacy. There was no prying, spying, or drama. I was grateful for that. I wasn't ready to talk. I needed time to recover, and they gave it to me.

The flurry of job offers confirmed what I'd always known but had never really acknowledged about myself: I was a valuable employee. I was reliable, hardworking, and loyal. In short, I was worth keeping around.

Someone in the radiology community threw a massive open house the next Christmas, a little over a year after I'd started my job. My bosses were unable to attend and asked me to go in their place. Most of the other guests were people I knew by name, if not in person. I made my rounds, spoke to everyone, made some friends, and was generally upbeat and congenial.

All that networking made me thirsty, so I headed off toward the buffet for something cool to drink. I served myself a glass of punch, lifted it to my lips, and almost choked. My old boss, the one who had fired me a few months before Tony's death, was standing a few feet away. "Carmen," she said. "Well, hello."

"H-hello," I stammered. "How are you?"

"Fine." We made small talk for about a minute in which we asked about each other's families. She swallowed. "I heard about your husband. I'm so sorry."

Something suddenly clicked for me. I still didn't understand why I'd had to lose my husband, but I did understand why I'd had to lose my job. This woman hadn't fired me because I was a bad employee. I suddenly realized why I'd been fired. "I'd never planned to see you again in this life," I told her, "but since we're here, I want to thank you. When you fired me, you gave me time with my husband. Back then, I didn't know how much that would matter to me, but now I'm grateful for it."

She gaped at me.

"So thank you," I reiterated. I was pleased to have the opportunity for some closure, which took another weight off my chest.

She blinked at the punch bowl. "I'll tell you what," she said, "if you're ever ready for another position in managerial work, call me." We both knew she didn't mean it. I think she was as surprised at the words coming out of her mouth as I was. Instead of laughing in her face, though, I dipped my head in thanks, and that was that.

# CHAPTER TWENTY-THREE

My life wasn't exactly smooth sailing after Tony's passing. I still felt the weight of his loss every day, but I no longer worried about feeding myself or paying my bills. I'd pulled out of my nosedive and had found some equilibrium despite my broken heart.

Ellie and I spent a day together in January of 2014. She was acting strangely, but I assumed it had something to do with her recent weight gain. She seemed very self-conscious about her body. As a kid, even in college, she'd always been petite. On our way home from lunch, I made a joking comment about her weight. She was gorgeous, so it seemed a silly thing to worry about. "Mom," Ellie blurted out, "I'm pregnant."

That seemed a lot less silly. I tightened my grip on the steering wheel. There was no sound in the truck except for the rumble of its engine.

"Mom," Ellie said, "say something."

I settled on saying, "I'm not as upset with you as the first time."

"Oh," she said. "Well, that's good…I guess."

We drove the rest of the way in awkward silence. Ellie probably thought I was giving her the silent treatment again, but I was wondering how we were going to get through this. When Nyla had been born, Tony and I had paid for everything. I couldn't do the same this time around. Now she would have to balance Nyla and a new baby instead of just Nyla. I wasn't angry, but I was overwhelmed with the amount of work we'd both have to do. When I stopped off at Ellie's place to let her out, I looked over. My daughter was sitting straight up in her seat. "Are you OK?" I asked.

She nodded, but just barely. "When Daddy was alive, I always felt safe. He'd never let anything happen to Nyla. He would've done anything for her." She put her hand over her belly and then launched out of the car before I could say a word. That was good. I had no idea what I could say to make things better.

I went home, sat down in Tony's favorite chair, and talked to him. I hoped he'd offer me some advice, although I wasn't sure how. When nothing happened, I went back into my room and turned on the TV. The Dallas Cowboys were on. Tony always loved the Cowboys. I heard a knock on the door. It was Little Tony. "Ma, can I come in?"

I switched off the TV and sat up. "Sure, baby. Come in."

Tony came into the bedroom and kissed me, the way he always did. He seemed preoccupied, and I wondered if Ellie had told him her news. Maybe he was worried that she and I had had another huge fight. "Ma, I need to talk," he said.

"So talk," I said, teasingly.

He paced back and forth across the room before he finally sat next to me. "Ma, I..." He was running his fingers through his hair, tapping his toes, and generally fidgeting. He sometimes got like this when he asked to borrow something, but I hoped it wouldn't be money. Just thinking about money made me tired.

"Spit it out," I said.

"My girlfriend's pregnant."

My head fell back against the pillow. *What next?*

"Ma, say something," he said, echoing his sister's words from earlier in the afternoon.

"Have you talked to Ellie?" I asked.

"No, why? What does she have to do with this?"

"Nothing." I stared at him. "This is a huge responsibility, you know?"

"I know," he said quickly. "I remember how you and Dad...I know this is a big deal."

"The biggest," I told him.

He nodded and seemed to be waiting for something else, maybe hoping I'd congratulate him. I didn't. I wasn't upset about the babies. What upset me was that Tony wasn't there, either to help or to celebrate. He would have been thrilled to have more kids around. As for me, I wasn't sure I remembered how to feel thrilled. More people to love only meant more heartbreak down the road. "I'll call you later," I said. "I need to think about this for a while."

"Are you angry?"

"No, I don't think so," I said. "Just worried."

"OK." He got up. "I love you, Ma."

"I love you, too."

He went to the door of my bedroom and then came back. "Ma," he asked, "are you afraid to die?"

I blinked at him. "No," I said. "When it's my time, I'll be with your father again. What about you? Are you afraid?"

Little Tony shook his head. "No. What's the point of being afraid? It happens to everyone." What had happened to my soft little boy who cried over television commercials? When had he become this matter-of-fact man? We'd all changed.

"Good night," I said. "We'll talk soon. I just need some time."

He nodded. I thought he might come back and kiss me good-bye, but instead he walked out of the room and left me alone.

I waited until I heard the door close before rolling over and staring at my husband's urn, which sat on a shelf beside the bed. "I know you had something to do with this baby business," I said.

I hadn't been involved in Ellie's first baby shower until the last minute, but the second time around I made up for it. I planned a double baby shower in honor of my two new grandchildren and put all my energy into making the event memorable. I wanted to show my children how much their happiness mattered to me. Their lives were different from the ones I'd have chosen for them, but they weren't my lives to live. Instead of worrying about the future, I embraced it. Those babies were blessings, and my children were happy.

I knew the shower would have mattered to Tony, too. I tried to bring as much enthusiasm to the event as he would have. That was a tall order, but I did my best. The baby shower was a huge outpouring of love. Friends, family, old clients—everyone wished my children well. I sat back and took a deep breath. Life would keep moving on, after all. We'd get better. We'd make new reasons to live.

Both mothers gave birth on Sundays when the Cowboys were playing. The Cowboys won both games. My daughter had been born on the twenty-eighth, and her second daughter was born on the twenty-eighth. My husband died on the twenty-eighth.

Tony had persuaded me to have a son who would carry on his name. Little Tony's first child was a boy, who could eventually do the same. Perhaps all this was random coincidence, but I don't believe in that.

My husband fought hard to come into this life, and after he left it, he gave me a few signs to let me know he hadn't disappeared completely. It was as if he'd reached out and shook me. He said in his usual blunt way, "Your children are happy, their children are healthy, and your life is still worth living, so it's time to cut the bullshit and move on."

# CHAPTER TWENTY-FOUR

**M**aybe my children and I have not moved on exactly, but we have moved forward since Tony's death. Little Tony is now the manager of a well-known Harlem restaurant famous for its Southern soul food. Ellie has owned and operated a beauty business for several years now. Initially she was, running a business that offered luxury hair styling, manicures, pedicures, and make-up applications at five star hotels. . She and her business partner had recently opened a physical location near Central Park.

When she told me she was expanding the business, I gave her a hug. "Now you can pay me back for your tuition!"

Ellie rolled her eyes. "You're funny, Mom."

"Yeah," I said, "but I'm serious, too."

She shook her head and sighed. "I know you are."

If I'd been able to map my kids' futures, I wouldn't have made all the same choices they have. Who knows what would have happened, though, if my father had made my choices for me? Life wasn't always easy for me, but I'm glad I had the freedom to choose my own way. My children are happy and successful—which is all I really wanted for them in the end.

Statistically speaking, my kids should be a mess, but they aren't. They're crazy, strong-willed, and hardworking people, just like their parents. I'm thankful that their temperaments are a little more refined than ours. They balance their emotions a little better than we ever did, although who knows where they learned that? Tony and I did the best we could and then stepped back to let them choose the next part.

Tony would have agreed: we did pretty well overall.

Tragedy teaches me who my friends are.

When I worked at the radiology lab downtown, I met a woman named Sara. We were friends, but I was never as close with her as I was with Ginger, Pat, or Marcia. After Tony's death, Sara came to check on me. I didn't know what to say, so the two of us sat in silence for a while. Eventually I cried. Sara just sat with me. She didn't try to calm me down or shut me up; she just kept me company. I blew my nose. "You don't have to do this, Sara," I told her.

"I don't mind."

Sara came once a week for a whole year, just to keep me company. Other friends called to express their sympathies, but Sara came there in person. Her presence and unhurried concern when she visited were beautiful gifts I might not have fully appreciated under other circumstances.

At the lowest point in my life, I really learned who was who. Tony's death taught me who and what was real. It meant a tremendous amount to me to have someone be so patient with my grief. It hadn't occurred to me that silence was what I needed until Sara offered me just that.

My other true friend in these last few years has been time. Some pain can't be fixed by anyone, but time takes the sharp edge off sorrow. The change in me was gradual. I didn't snap out of my slump completely, but I have escaped from the fog.

Grief, although it hurt, taught me what's important to me. I've shifted my priorities. I have a new perspective and have learned not to take anything for granted. The time that separates me from my lowest point has made day-to-day living easier, while the time still ahead of me has gained new significance. I have to make it count.

I always believed I had a purpose. Why else would I be born after my mother thought she was done with babies? Tony had a purpose, too. Why else would he have survived his childhood illness?

For years, my purpose in life was to influence Tony to be a better man, and I did. We bettered each other. That was part of his purpose—to smooth my edges, calm my temper, and help me be a better version of myself. My purpose in his life is done, but his effect on me is still taking place. If I can't be there for Tony, then I have to find another way to leave a positive foot-print on this world.

I now manage two radiology labs, and my son and I have opened a small business on the side. We work as private consultants, sometimes for businesses, some-times for individuals. I do most of my work in lab or office settings, and Little Tony specializes in restau-rant consultation. He's especially interested in helping young men take control of their futures. His father was passionate about this issue, and our son carries on that passion.

Part of my job involves fixing résumés, conduct-ing mock interviews, and providing personal con-sultations. Most clients are willing to work hard, but they need modeling on how to make a good first im-pression or to maintain a professional attitude in the workplace. My job is to help people feel secure in their abilities and to deliver a better service experience to their customers and clients.

Our business is called R.A. W Consulting—*ready and willing*. That was the name of Tony's barbershop, and although we no longer have the shop, the name feels like a good omen. It's a gift from my husband, who was always ready and willing to take on the next challenge.

As satisfying as it is to see nervous clients build their confidence or watch a struggling business right itself, that's not enough. I want to find a way to change people's lives when they need it most. Tony came in to save me once, back when I really needed it. I've laid out a plan for a foundation to empower young women, especially those who face domestic violence. I want to provide young women with information about where to go for counseling and to provide disenfranchised kids with after-school services and access to day trips out of the city. When people see that there's more to life than what's in front of them, they can imagine a broader future for themselves.

All my experiences, good and bad, woke me up to the fact that life is too short to spend on complaining. I need to do the next thing, and I need to be grateful for what I have. I've always been a fighter, but anyone can learn to fight for themselves. They just have to believe their lives, dreams, and futures are worth the fight.

Every year, Tony's birthday and the anniversary of his death make two weeks of June hard for the kids and me to bear. Instead of sitting around and feeling the heartbreak, we find a few days so that we can all go away together for an adventure. I mix in the painful memories of loss with the creation of new and beautiful experiences. Sometimes we go to an exotic location such as Aruba, and sometimes to a more rustic setting like the Catskills. We do a lot of crying, but we also do plenty of laughing. We can't let grief overtake us, or we'd lose track of the joy we feel about all the things we still have.

The Lord doesn't dole out more than anyone can handle. If I'd been able to guess my own future, I would have been wrong about how things turned out, but this was what had to happen. Tony's death bent and crippled me, but it didn't break me. I came back stronger. I persevered because I knew I had a purpose to fulfill.

When Ellie opened the physical location of her beauty salon, she ordered a set of refurbished iPads for the employees. The day they arrived, she came to see me, absolutely hysterical. "What's wrong, honey?" I asked as she bawled beside me on the couch.

She handed me an iPad. I examined it, not sure of what I was supposed to see. "Turn it over," she said, sobbing.

I did and discovered an engraving on the back: *To my fabulous daughter. Love, Dad.*

I held Ellie close. Some people might call it a random coincidence, but my daughter doesn't believe in happenstance. And neither do I. I miss Tony every day, but I know he's with us. He's rooting for us. He gives us signs.

Back when we first lived together, before we were married, Tony liked to ask me big "if" questions: *If you could go anywhere on the planet, where would you go? If you could do whatever you wanted without worrying about the cost, what would you do?* One night, as we lay in our bed, Tony asked me, "If you could have anything in the world, what would it be?"

I rested my head on his shoulder and thought about it. "I don't know."

"Oh, come on." He rolled over, grinning down at me. "If I said, 'Ma, I'll give you anything you want,' what would you ask for?"

When he put it that way, it was much easier to answer. "You."

He wiggled his eyebrows at me.

"Really," I insisted. "There's nothing you can buy me that I can't buy myself. But you can give me your heart only if you want to."

"Easy," he said, and he kissed me. "You already have it."

True love might not always look like a fairy tale, but I know it's real. I've felt it. Sometimes it's frustrating and sometimes it's painful. Sometimes you want to smack the other person upside the head and ask him what he was thinking. Sometimes one of you goes to jail or the other ends up estranged from most of her family. Sometimes, despite the true love, the fridge is bare. That doesn't make the love any less true.

Everything happens for a reason. We are each given a purpose, even if we don't know what that purpose is. It's not always easy—I've gotten lost more than once in my life. But I got lucky, too. Tony and I collided, and we knew from the day we met that our purposes were wrapped up in themselves.

Two unlikely people came into this world fighting, and we found what some people look for their whole lives. We found real love.

# ACKNOWLEDGMENTS

**Ellie and Little Tony**—Better versions of your dad and me, you two gave us a chance to experience one of the greatest gifts on earth. My love for you allowed me to overcome many difficult times. You always kept me focused, and when things didn't go well, I always thought of what my mom told me: "Those kids did not ask to be in this world." I wanted better for both of you, and I knew I had to give you that chance. I hope you are as proud of me as I am of you. We have an unbreakable bond that will always keep us together. I love you the most.

**Nyla, Roclyn, and Trey**—"Other Mommy" loves you all tremendously. Thank you for bringing me happiness during a dark part of my life. I am sorry you never got the chance to really know Poppa, but he lives within us all. He would have spoiled you beyond your parents' understanding. I love you.

**My mother**—Thank you for showing me what class and grace look like. You taught me at a very early age to always help others, and although most people never noticed, I was your Number one student. Thank you for passing on those beautiful genes of grace, kindness, loyalty, and integrity. I am very proud of all those traits. I miss and love you very much.

**My other half**—I miss you, my number one fan, every single moment of every single day. I hope you are proud. When I told you all those years ago, "I think I want to write a book," without hesitation, you responded, "Go for it. You can do anything." Thank you for listening, teaching, caring, and especially for loving me for who I am and never, ever trying to change me. You treated me with respect and truly cared about my feelings. I know you've carried me these last four years since your death and that you'll continue to do so in the future. Although you are no longer here physically, I am still in love with you. When we first dated and I told you I loved you, your response was always the same: "What is love?" My face had a distorted look the first time you said that, so you added, "Love is the highest degree of elevation, and we're not there yet." Years later you said, "Ma, we're there," and I said, "Yes, we are." My heart will forever be broken, but I thank God I experienced what many people search their entire lives for—real love. Until we meet again, I will do my best to leave my imprint on this world.

**Marcia**—Thank you for being my friend when I was on lockdown, for never making fun of my restrictions, and especially for sharing your beautiful mother with me. As we always said, we're not friends—we're family. I love you and the entire Johnson family forever.

**Richie**—They branded us "unwanted ones." Thank you for being my brother/sister. You've always stood by me, even when you thought I was going crazy. Thank you for loving me without judgment and especially for helping me with Ellie and Tony when I was alone. I am forever thankful for everything you've done for my family and me. I love you always.

**To the rest of my family and friends**—Thank you for all your kindness and support over the years. I am truly grateful.

**To those who have wronged me**—Life is too short to hold bitterness, anger, or revenge. Whatever you might have done in the past, I forgive you. I learned a lesson even during those dark times.

To learn more about Carmen Ashe, share a story, or to contact the author for a speaking engagement, please visit her website:

Ihaveapurpose.com.

# ABOUT THE AUTHOR

It took Carmen Ashe more than seven years to share her story. *I Have a Purpose* is an inspirational and encouraging true tale that confronts every obstacle she's encountered, from the tragedy of abuse and loss to the triumph of true love and happiness. It is a testimony of Carmen's dedication to her family as well as of her faith and determination to face life's challenges, stand up for what she believes in, and never give up, no matter what.

Carmen lives in New York near her beloved adult children. She owns a consulting firm and also contributes to her community by bringing her story of strength to those who may have lost hope as a demonstration that everyone has a purpose in life.

Made in the USA
Columbia, SC
13 September 2018